The Jolly Rubino

Rubino del Sur

Histericks 24

Bio: Rubino was the name of a French colonel, an employee of the French West African Company (CFAO), massacred during the revolt of Abés in 1910 in the village that bears his name. His tomb became a historical site open to the public years later. During the colonization of Côte d'Ivoire by France, the resistance of the Abbey to French settlers from 1905 to 1918 peaked in1910. Colonel Rubino, was murdered in recurring raids on the settlers, his body cooked and settlers made to eat the dish. The city became a place of pilgrimage to the mausoleum of Rubino. The present day physiologist of this name who continues to write telling on the various identities of urinary speech in those bases of the west of modern constituency.

He invented the *chattel binding branch of experimental dentistry,* those Maquilas teeth of invisible servitude and served in capacities in the States where his offenses were less known. He now works at McMurdo Station. A citizen of three nations, first born Argentine, he was made British through the Penal citizenship program at Pentonville which provided his education in dentistry. Emerging, he continued at York and Sussex U's in jaw formation of hybrid and synthetic speech to such a degree that·after the Eau Claire Mayo, the Clinic at Denai, and Fukushima Prefecture he became a U.S. citizen with corporate status, being his third passport, to train, and embark to his present location where he combines propitiatory experiment in Nano-composites, Synthesis of Grafted Polymer Speech to Text, Text to Speech, and Hybrid Environments in Primate skull morphology on a contract basis. He is a palantirologist of soccer. His alternate being Rubion del Sure. He has contributed to the Rueben Crater. Rubino has lately documented examinations of faciation zones in the Chernobyl mind which emerged in the irradiated writing following these exposures. To show how the head has been made subordinate to the vertebrate as a pharyngeal twist of the science of linguistics in the jawbone of these affairs, Rubino published Notes To the Earth Orcprothangon in the Evolutionary Dentation Trends and Scutes of Oraclar Subclades as well as some of the lost letters of Freud, and an anthropology study of Sasquatch, along with other works.

Contents

Acknowledgments to *Unlikely Stories 2.0* and for providing off shoots of *Playdate* by a known author, and to *Mannequin Haus* for the superb layout of *Murder of the World*, now, *Jolly* and *Join the Brigades.* Brigades also appeared at *Unlikely*. Fry Brain, September, Headless Mountain were at *Anvil Tongue,* 2021.Eventually the result of politics and murder gibberish in Rubino here include *Sasquatch* at *The Gambler Mag*, 2017 and *Subfornical Organ*, the lost letters of Freud at *Squawk Back*, 2017. We do not conclude with Black Hole Down that first was at *Antipodean SF. -Italics show Blake, Shakespeare and anon. All this is how we think of the Wreck of the Hesperus and the Wreck of the Deutschland with the Jolly Rubino as the ship of state*

The Reptilican Convention

Of Cleveland 2016

They raise their heads on caucus stalks,
those fgov aliens made of pot,
Seven ballots take the crown
that time warp bands Reptile around.

The best kept dragon sulphurity
Of insects fracked July.
Rub with garlic to purify.

On Wal-Mart! Ohio,
Pittsburgh lament
the brazen sea that culled our House!
That people sprayed to Oz.

Akron was drawn to afterlife
And Cleveland beat its breast.
Cleveland!

There goes Shaker Heights into the sea!
Top priests wrote convention blurbs
that let the future out.
Driven by Chicago's Stress
pyramids and mounds
a 9self formulated id broke skin.

New York, Darjeeling, east LA,
buried sin to place the blame,
Japan went to the sun with the D.C. mayor.

Marduke at the Capitol
and Merkel shot a round.
Fish, fowl and beast creep to the stars,
and Nineveh bowled the aisle.

Graft Maple, Oak and iron then
to ten million men with brains,
Kedar, Edom, Bobal bloom.
Reptilians just stayed home.

A deeper frack of Cleveland hit

when aliens played it long.

Want transcendence?

Scabbers scrape their knees

To transcendent corporate Babylon.

No wonder Thought Goats praise.

No wonder Ezekiel had passengers hold their nose.

Caligula practiced global scale

To smoke the Schumann Rez,

Soaked in brandy, sliced to rounds,

dried in sugar, nominations lunge

the hyper hermetic Tree.

Do you want knowledge, do you want power? IED to fairy tale.

Akron and Gaza would not dry out.

Manhattan not drive out its doubt,

L.A. worshipped the stars.

The convention was a Security Event

necessary to save the president.
Transcendent terrorists
rolled their lungs.
Or roll your own
Man mountain myths
for reservations argue
shock and awe on homeland north
would wake the merchant stars.

Global captives shook
transcendence first.

No enemy wants to eat that fig
the men of No-Cleveland bought and sold.
Dissenting reptiles sang this song
that dawn with chains of concrete bongs.

Concrete pop!
Space-garde Weiner
schnitzel mas!
Infra mutants

Ghibboleth.
If this seems plyed with intelliars,
technique consciousness, mystery plates,
where Secret Service weld blood rites
to nucleotides, then

Join the

Brigades!

"Say now Shibboleth: and he said Siboleth,
for he could not frame it right." *Judges*. 12.6

@ Join the Brigades Quinhaus 10, Neon Garden & Unlikely Stories

Mark V

SEPTEMBER

We have to bypass thought to think
What’s sleeping in our mind.
Do something warns the empty thought
September overwhelms.

Against these harbingers Pentagon,
Males Millennium and Tribulation one,
to reconstruct complete bete noir
in the warehouse of the mind.

The King mass corp of new techniques
new conquerors took control,
in subclade Scales Imperials debate
how Incompleteness would close.

UN Prisoner Transfer cars resettled to the east,
the Unity State took cargo loads
of animated beasts.

Guns in the bedroom, one under the chair,
guns in the fridge and in bête noire
the old warehouse of the mind.
Days before the Flood we thought
to topple kings of war
before Impossibilities taught
do not be one with the world.

Scientificos would CRISPR you
At Lunch with Baal Peor.
Sheol is bigger from reflux!
Eyes ope' and ears can hear
the expansion of Sheol.

Indian, Irish, German, Black
against the English caught
Christian between new life and flesh;
We knew it as we walked.

LOOK UP HEADLESS

What is wilderness? I will tell!
Wilderness glistens beneath a bear
which opens up its mouth. Its tail is a crowd
of bones inside of subway tubes.
Come and capture. Pierce the nose!
There is a bronze wake underside
that leaves a trail.
Think the waves are cedar?
lie down upon a tongue leash for girls,
Make a treaty fire on a row of shields,
Harpoon the head you mountaineers!
Strip off its coat, take light as your own,

"Where are you, I am looking."
When we look up headless
to see what topknots know,
Ride the mirror to the back of it
For the face is the eye seen through,
The face of mountain is a mask
That hunts for eye and ear,
The head remains embodied earth

To raise a tongue for headless eyes to watch
the hunt for elk and quartz.

Ichabod Crane has a shoulder there
Beneath the pie bald sky.
Not really Danes, cold mouths devour
The rooster tail stuck to mouth.
Rock towers ask, "enemy or friend?"
As the angel said to Joshua and Joshu then.

Where are you hiding mule deer among
the bone-flushed xylene pumps
in a pile of cans full of sin?

Rock against fish, prison against Fox,
Civilization's four wheel government
are mine to hunt Behemoth.
Warm and bored in bed
lassoed saguaros, shot and hung to dry,
Bodies were everywhere in the spirit wild.

Design the crotch?
Heavy petting is a letting go.
Do not leave prairie
Or pretend not one remains.

A hundred versions of Opiomes
blamed Coleridge for the Trojan Horse
stabled in Denver's bat cave,
home of the Broncos and Pegasus
where Mustang Sally became one
Vision of the Starchitect Hotel became myth
in the spit of Jonathan Swift.

2nd Early Tattooed High Govt Habit Swine Fry Flu Release

We who search the headless top
From the mirror on the back

of mountain in a mask
That hunts for ear and eye.
believe the Ants had too much high
aluminum today.
Do you see in the sunny grid
where woodpeckers hover
& black bumbles stumble,
the gold where the peckers are pecking?
That ain't all you got with Fry Flue brain,
To peck on your knot again,
the Russians woodpeckers and dudder physics,
hatching little godlings on the griddle,
scalar wrong to be soon changed
is in the conifer off *grid raising*
A menagerie of gophers to attack the poles
in the 2nd ed release
of early tattooed high govt fry brain.

Grasshoppers swipe the gibber code,

To tape record video,
Freedom of Thought Information dreams
nouns and verbs cut off dissociation
that beat the MMPI
make a **hyno**-program courier.
An NLP toolbox stole microwave,
Of magnetic hypothesis recall mop up
Experimentation slabs
bank left and right, new technique
final interview tonight.

"How does it feel during the search ?
Did it rain? Do you remember the command
beginning electronic dissolution of memory?
Was erased two dimensional tactile kinesthetic.
politician got the flu,
Psycho science gives the second signal now.
One Hundred Thousand codes,
replaced Mind Control.

Hypno-programmed NLP defense,
Adversity therapy, Eureka pleasure release.

In the war against George Romney,
Imagination, Jack Ruby, National Security,
Dept of Energy, fusion energy, General Atomics,
fusion orbit, spider web satellite tech,
quarantined pygmy speech, red herring each
fake Grey abduction and stun gun amnesia,
Screen scrambles, ritual deficit disorder, armies
scramble, MPD military **hypno**-courier.
Military passified spychiatrists,
Delta Force Waco code trigger verse,
in 10 minutes, dissociate and look.

Brain tuner, sound color, monarchist
psychocivilized soc,
needles through skull, Parkinson's, magnetic
manipulate EMR,

TP, test person, Mendocino Mental.
Janet Reno, Anthony Robbins,
meet the mind brainwash,
patsy **hypno**-programmed Sirhan rapport.
Elsberg, Nixon, Leary cryptocrat,
presidential model hypnosis.
Ear receivers, ping pong eyes,
mad scientist white sound
drum sense ever cease to civ.
All news, every station Crypotech,
Carl Nicholi, NSA stunt Act.
Inalienable right, 2nd ed release early tattooed
high govt habit swine fry release flu.

Coronavirus and Twin Towers Theatre: Dean Kootz, James Laughlin

These exercises in **Opaque pattern recognition** are calculated along with lies. Every trigger event is contrived. We just don't know how to do it. Who knows what insights might occur by spreading a wide net in the oddities of literature?

There the headlines of the Daily Express say in the fiction of Dean Koontz, "new biological weapon" created by a Chinese scientist to "wipe out a city or country" a bio weapon man-made microorganism called “Wuhan-400” with transmission possible without symptoms. “They call the stuff ‘Wuhan-400’ because it was developed at their RDNA labs outside the city of Wuhan and it was the 400th viable strain of man-made microorganisms created at that research centre." Are we reading fiction or is fiction veiling news? US Senator Tom Cotton read Koontz too, claimed it was either an experiment gone wrong, or a purposely released biological weapon.

A lot of effort continues to deny that **fiction predicted Covid-19 virus and poetry predicted the fall of the Twin Towers**. What other events are predicted ahead in drama? Most of these occur in film where writers and predictive events are smoking Nostradamus. Those writers have ahold of a list of script scenarios of the future, one or all of which play out, that science fiction writers got from the occult. It's not an act of imagination, or science fiction. It's a script. After you have seen how frequent these are you can begin.

Contexts

In the film *Armageddon* (1998) World Trade Center towers appear on the screen greatly damaged from having been hit by asteroids. At another point a space ship countdown clock is shown stuck in the “9:11” position. And consider “Neo's,” passport in *Matrix* showing an expiration date of September 11, 2001 or Ben Affleck's character's eye exam in Pearl harbor (1999) reads a clear "911." All these are susceptible to the fact check nits in general and Wendell Berry in particular about the towers (below)

The Pearl Harbor event itself, of course, was supposed and presented as a surprise military strike against the US by the Imperial Japanese. Ha. Ha, just the way all over children's books and comic books languishes the saga of the tsunami folded $20 bill. Whether the coincidence of numbers 33 with geographical parallels correlates I Ching with the Chinese language, Mayan Calendar, Hopi Blue Star, Niburu, Richard Hoagland's take on the Mars escapees, abductees on Iapetus, channeled and rechanneled gibberings of Isis, more alarmed abductees (Recall, 2017) right out of Professor David Jacobs of the hybid *Threat* (1998) and other works on the hybrid scientist lab rat-bred government agent disinformings, or none, are offered for consumption.

Dean Kootz, starts off coronovirus in *The Eyes of Darkness*. According to these Conspiracies fact checking at Menu says what twitter reported early, but humorless debunking is too literal minded to miss the grand scheme. In its debunking it sounds completely like Wendell Berry's debunk of James **Laughlin's** (publisher of New Directions Press) "Above the City" a poem of 1946 *predicting* the fall of the Twin Towers (2001). And both of these instances can either be taken as myth and further myth or vaunted illumined boast tips required before administration of such events, implying a much greater footing in the America in the Bible plan. Leave the plan aside right now and examine the conditions.

Fact checkers say:

"The Eyes of Darkness," a science fiction novel written by Dean Koontz and published in 1981.references a fictional "biological weapon" called "Wuhan-400" that was designed to kill people but inadvertently gives one child's psychic abilities. The real coronavirus in Wuhan (technically known as "SARS-CoV-2", which causes the disease now known as "Covid-19") and this fictional weapon have little in common, except they both occur in the Chinese city of Wuhan. In the book, the fictional disease was developed at "labs outside the city of Wuhan". The real outbreak of Covid-19 is believed to have originated in the city.

As we've written about before, there's no evidence that Covid-19 was artificially created, or originated from a lab [which means of course there is lots!]

Other characteristics of "Wuhan-400" don't match Covid-19. The book says that "Once infected, no one lives more than twenty-four hours" and that its "kill-rate is one hundred percent", something that is not true of Covid-19, which has a fatality rate of around 2%. [Good news, huh?]

The book also says that it "afflicts only human beings" and that "no other living creature can carry it", while Covid-19 is believed to have crossed over into humans from bats, possibly via a third animal. [Eat a bat raw and a little snake in your soup to prove it.]

And Covid-19 is a respiratory disease, while the book's disease affects the brain stem, where it "begins secreting a toxin that literally eats away brain tissue like battery acid dissolving cheesecloth." ["The infection of SARS-CoV has been reported in the brains from both patients and experimental animals, where the brainstem was heavily infected. "] https://www.the-scientist.com/features/can-the-flu-and-other-viruses-cause-neurodegeneration--65498

The other book the Daily Star mentions is called "End of Days: Predictions and prophecies about the end of the world" co-written by "psychic and spiritual teacher" Sylvia Browne, and published in 2008. It claims: "In around 2020 a severe pneumonia-like illness will spread throughout the globe, attacking the lungs and the bronchial tubes and resisting all known treatments." It's worth noting that, while there is not yet a vaccine for the Covid-19 coronavirus, the human immune system does fight the disease. As noted, most victims survive. Trials of vaccines and other potential treatments are currently underway. It's also worth noting that this prediction was made just a few years after the (closely related) SARS outbreak, and that it comes amidst some of the book's other health predictions—which include claiming a cure for "paralysis and Parkinson's disease [will be found] no later than 2012", and the assertion that "blindness will become a thing of the past by 2020". So much for the false facts and assumed facts. Pay the drones.

A Tale of Two Towers

But in the poem the Empire State Building gets hit by a plane in 1945. Laughlin watches it from his office in the Salmon Tower (1930) a 58-story tower the immediate precursor to the Empire State Building built the next year by the same architects. (The Midtown Book) immediate precursor of the Empire State Building (1931) of 102 stories The significance is not in the details but the embellishment. It is Saturday morning in the poem. They are working in a matter of fact tone, "finishing up some late invoices." The writer sees a plane, which he calls a bomber because it is a bomber in the news. Like an apparition it "roars through the mist" and crashes as if by implication into the Empire State. Flames pour from the windows after the explosion. The "two paragons of progress," either the airplane and the building, or by extension the two buildings, "perform before our eyes their true relationship," that is, *they fall.* It's almost as if alternate futures revealed themselves but only sometimes were recognized. Is it easier to believe the 1946 crash and the 2001 were random events or that the conspirators knew of the previous crash and copied it? It is as if every news account were capable of bearing future analogues that history does or does not repeat.

The 58 story Salmon Tower was the tallest building in New York City prior to the North Tower of the World Trade Center of 1972.

"You're never going to be any good as a poet," Ezra Pound told James Laughlin, publisher of New Directions Press, but nobody said he couldn't be a prophet. Wendell Berry claimed Laughlin's "Above the City" of 1946 *accidently predicted* the fall of the Twin Towers of 2001. Nassim Taleb claimed he did *not* predict 9/11 either, even if his *Fooled by Randomness*, published a week before 9/11, said a plane could crash into an office building. Various psychic spies claim they knew whatever. That Nostradamus knew. That the Feds knew, CIA knew, but back on Mount Olympus the blind Oedipus kings couldn't see. The fact checkers claim with careful selection of their details, claim poets aren't prophetic even *after* the event. They cite that Keats claimed Cortez, not Balboa, discovered the Pacific!

Poet Wendell Berry doubts the McLaughlin prophet. He stands in for government doubters of the prophet events of Ground Zero. "It is tempting to call this poem prophetic," he says. "but it is only so in the sense that it is insightful; it perceives the implicit contradiction between tall buildings and airplanes. This contradiction was readily apparent also to the terrorists of September 11, but evidently invisible within the mist of technological euphoria that had surrounded the great innovators and decision makers" (*Citizenship Papers*, 2003, 98).

Berry, like the Greeks, makes it a moral lesson on blindness, as if poets are better at morality than Keats at history, "the results of great decisions not adequately informed" (99). In addition to tall buildings he fears for nuclear power plants and a food supply system threatened with bioterrorism as much as others might fear the fall of the dollar, unemployment and the housing market. He calls it a failure of the "rational mind." But the problem of predicted events is how far out they occur.

To be valuable prediction has to fall in a window of usefulness. Knowing a rise in the price of gold, the market up or down, depression or war is only valuable in a lifetime. It does no good after. Pundits predict commodities, but not assassinations, floods, earthquakes. Those are for prophets. The medievals prophesied by the three Ds, death, decay, disease. If Laughlin's 1946 prophetic journalism predates its historical fulfillment and he and we don't know he's doing it, what good is it? Oh Cassandra!

There are three direct correlations with the literal towers in the poem, Salmon Tower and Empire State, furthered by their being called "two paragons," that make the insight:

1) It isn't just an airplane, it's "*a bomber.*"
2) When it strikes the Empire State Building in the poem, "*flames poured from the windows*," exactly what happened at the explosion of the fuel tanks.
3) "*Sirens screamed down in the streets below*," closely resembling the call in which 341 firefighters died, along with the massive police and EMS response:

But if the literal denies the symbolic the Tower guy gets taken away:

--"The details are wrong. It wasn't the *18th floor*. The South Tower was hit above the 86th floor, the North Tower above the 96th

--It wasn't *Saturday morning*, it was Tuesday.

--The "bomber" was really an airliner, two of them.

--The World Trade Center didn't exist in 1946. It opened in 1970. The two towers in Laughlin's poem, Salmon Tower and Empire State, are not "twin towers."

--The collision of “two paragons of progress” in Laughlin’s poem is literally a poetic commentary on an actual collision of a B-25 bomber that crashed into the 79th floor of the Empire State Building 28 July 1945. It can almost be seen live: “Bomber Hits Skyscraper in Heavy Fog.”

Eventualities and Incongruities

All of this can come under the heading of eventualities and incongruities that occur when “the great innovators and decision makers build huge airplanes whose loads of fuel make them, in effect, flying bombs. And they build the World Trade Center, forgetting apparently the B-25 bomber that crashed into the seventy-ninth floor of the Empire State Building in 1945. And then on September 11, 2001 some enemies--of a kind we well knew we had and evidently had decided to ignore--captured two huge airplanes and flew them, as bombs, into the two towers of the World Trade Center. In retrospect, we may doubt that those shaping decisions were properly informed, just as we may doubt that the expansive “intelligence” that is supposed to foresee and prevent such disasters is sufficiently intelligent” (Berry, 97).

When Berry is done we don’t feel so bad, because he affirms the subtext of the official reports that it’s all been a mistake that nobody could have foreseen, with no suggestion of a divine or human mousetrap.

The Myth

Not all news accounts are as prophetic as a B-25 bomber awaiting time and place, but who thinks ahead and changes their behavior on the basis of a past event? Nobody. Instead they wait for the event to happen and react, but not ahead of time. To further Berry’s rationalisms, it seems inevitable that in millenniums ahead the tale of two towers will be compared to myth, taken as allegory and doubted as fact.

Can you imagine what the architects will say? Reduced to interpretation, there may be little difference then between news accounts and archeological speculations about ziggurats on Babylon's plain, excavations of Troy VIIA and the Fall of Babel, a "story possibly… inspired by the fall of the famous temple-tower of Etemenanki." The towers will symbolize Ilium and the dissolution of the Ring. New York, Troy-Babel, will show the limit of reason. Beowulf, Faustus, Milton, Blake imprisoned in the stone where Merlin lay as a symbol of the brain, will, with venetian blinds, vinyl chairs and the prescience of technology show poets as the unacknowledged journalists of the world!

Thus symbol before and after the fact will be explained as either natural cause or symbolic, whether 3000 or 60 years separate the two. The Judgment of nations and Greek fate that strikes Lycidas with the blinded fury of the anointed spear and Oedipus can do nothing but be driven by his hubris to his fate, and kings will make mistakes because of their *good intent or pride* and have their eyes put out, or dreams and omens vex the court of King Arthur and the courts of a nation, we shall insist are two different things.

That's the way it goes in the duality world, paradox revels of entertainment. *Te deum deus ex machina* should not dare to appear in current events! Government, industry, academia and all world powers oppose this understanding. There can be no such thing as fate, destiny or judgment, judgment for sin, *hamartia*, hubris overreaching.

Fate is not a topic of journalism but of demonic literature, as if fate put current events causes taken as hysteria, as if the thoughts of madmen were broadcast over the news, except these thoughts *are* now broadcast over mainstream, and the more scripted, repetitive and partisan the more it passes for discourse. Against this backdrop fate hands out omens.

Presidents and architects of drones strike appreciate nuance. It's as if a missile were launched on the other side of the world to strike at the symbolic heart of the American government, which depending on the day, would be due either to constituted right or commercial power. Taking the case, the missile *airpliances* stuck unknowing, *ewhich* just happened to be in this first inaugural spot of the first president. Call it collateral damage. What American drones do in Pakistan or Afghanistan is called the fog of war. When the Federal Hall was awash in ash it was dismissed and the promise was to rebuild bigger and stronger, so as not to seem to have been defeated. But governments do not believe in the judgement of God on them, they believe in their judgement upon their enemies. So even if there were omissions and failures in Benghazi, or 9/11, or… no natural event is symbolic, it is explained away as effectively as Wendell Berry does McLaughlin.

But journalism catches up to lit. Trayvon Martin was "a sacrifice for all of us." "Zimmerman doesn't last a year till the hood catches up to him," Victor Cruz of the of the NBC Giants said. Roddy White of the CNN Falcons said, "them jurors should go home tonight and kill themselves for letting a grown man get away with killing a kid." Abortion became such an act of heroism for human rights in New York that you could be killed in the womb the second before you were born. Pornography raised the banner of free speech. Gay marriage was the liberation of hope.

When Jerry Falwell seemed to say the day after that 9/11 was the judgment of God people went as nuts as when Michelle Bachmann repeated it a decade later and added Benghazi of 9/11/12 to the list. None of these events produced regret in the pundits or the government, just the opposite, they swole up. To them the judgment of God was a right-wing plot.
Why then do the nations so furiously rage together, the people imagine a vain thing?

"We explain the phenomenon it forces on our minds as a truth which the incurably evolutionary or developmental character of modern thought is always urging us to forget. What is vital and healthy does not necessarily survive. Higher organisms are often conquered by lower ones...an art, a whole civilization, may at any time slip through mens' fingers in a very few years and be gone beyond recovery.
If we are alive when such a thing is happening we shall hardly notice it until too late; and it is most unlikely that we shall know its causes."

.(C. S. Lewis. *English Literature in the Sixteenth Century*, 113).

Above the City

You know our office on the 18th
floor of the Salmon Tower looks
right out on the

Empire State and it just happened
we were there finishing up some
late invoices on

a new book that Saturday morning
when a bomber roared through the
mist and crashed

flames poured from the windows
into the drifting clouds and sirens
screamed down in

the streets below it was unearthly
but you know the strangest thing
we realized that

none of us were much surprised because we'd always known that those

two paragons of

progress sooner or later would perform before our eyes this demon-
stration of their
true relationship.

Things thought and impossible to say, to give ten minutes to one who comes to the threshold before sudden crossing. I want ten minutes for him to see what he thought was against what was so all along. This, from one who shares the concern, about the **"sudden extinction of a poetical literature"** in Scotland.

"However we explain the phenomenon, it forces on our minds a truth which the incurably evolutionary or developmental character of modern thought is always urging us to forget. What is vital and healthy does not necessarily survive. Higher organisms are often conquered by lower ones...an art, a whole civilization, may at any time slip through mens' fingers in a very few years and be gone beyond recovery. IF WE ARE ALIVE WHEN SUCH A THING IS HAPPENING WE SHALL HARDLY NOTICE IT UNTIL TOO LATE; AND IT IS MOST UNLIKELY THAT WE SHALL KNOW ITS CAUSES." Lewis, *Sixteenth Century*, 113.

Israel Kryptonite

All these events are scripted in advance and given a tip of the hat to assure the commoner of the shock and awe that surrounds. It makes you feel just like a Viet Cong soldier, an Iraqi Baathist, an

Afghan *mujahideen*, a Mennonite. These political bodies implicate all. September 12, 2001, Tom Daschle, Senate Majority Leader, introduced a **joint resolution** condemning the attacks with emphasis that he spoke for all, both houses and parties. He likewise linked his remarks to the Republic's founding 212 years before for four blocks from Ground Zero was the site of the first American capitol and the first inauguration of George Washington in 1789. Daschle did not know how far the **"symbols and structures of our economic and military strength"** were compromised on purpose. He was not aware at all when he linked America with ancient Israel in the prophecy of Isaiah that instead of "God bless the people of America" he was delivering a curse.

"It is with pain, sorrow, anger and resolve that I stand before this Senate, assembled for **212 years** of the strength of our democracy and say that America will emerge from this tragedy as we have emerged from all adversity, united and strong. The America in which we woke today is far different from the one in which we woke yesterday. This morning as our rescue workers and medical personnel continue their heroic work we begin to truly understand **the enormity** of what happened. My heart aches for the people of New York, our men and women serving at the Pentagon, the passengers and crew of the four hijacked aircraft and for their families and friends. These attacks were an assault on our people and on our freedom. They aimed at **the heart of the American community and the symbols and structures of our economic and military** strength. As an American, as an elected representative I am outraged, as a husband, as a father I am pained beyond words. Last night we sent a message to the world that even in the face of such cowardly and heinous acts the doors of democracy will not close. **This joint resolution** we lay down today condemns yesterday's attacks, expresses our sympathy for the victims and our support for the president as our commander in chief. The world should know that the **members of both parties** in both houses stand united in this. The full resources of our government will be brought to bear in aiding the search and rescue and in hunting down those responsible and those who may have aided or harbored them. Nothing, nothing can replace the losses of those that have suffered.

I know that there is only the smallest measure of inspiration that can be taken from this devastation. But there is a passage in the Bible from Isaiah that I think speaks to us all at times like this. **'The bricks have fallen down but we will rebuild with dressed stone; the fig trees have been felled but we will replace them with cedars.'** That is what we will do. We will rebuild and we will recover, the people of America will stand strong together because the people of America have always stood together. And those of us privileged to serve this great nation will stand with you. God bless the people of America." here

Isaiah spoke these words in the moment of the Assyrian assault, when Jerusalem's buildings and towers fell, its trees cut and it vowed to rebuild better, stronger that before.
How exactly this spells out in coming years, through the market meltdown that came seven years later, and what would come in seven more years at 2015 is left to its own surmise. J Cahn has laid it out.

The first to suggest Isaiah the biblical prophet predicts 9/11 isn't a preacher, but the senate majority leader after 9/11, Tom Daschle, and the commissions of site restoration of Ground Zero, the ones who put in the hewn stone, and lowered the cedar into the sycamore's hole. all different agencies in this case, but the overall attitude of the restoration was shared by them all, from Bush to Obama recently, who wrote on the beam, "We remember We rebuild We come back stronger." I don't make this stuff up. I saw them, Giant boots began to tramp back and forth across the country... **IF WE ARE ALIVE WHEN SUCH A THING IS HAPPENING WE SHALL HARDLY NOTICE IT UNTIL TOO LATE; AND IT IS MOST UNLIKELY THAT WE SHALL KNOW ITS CAUSES..."** making holes and shallows and swamps and thumps but no one could see above the tops. I have said over and over again that "depressions left by their feet in the park drowned little dogs." Now you know what they are.

The kryptonite of Israel was the attitude that it would *defy* its enemy, because the defiance was really against Yahweh. Isaiah makes this clear. He shouts Isaiah 9.10 at them, says that they might say they will replace the bricks with hewn stone, the sycamore's with cedar and built ever stronger and bigger, but they won't. Hewn stone is celebrated as being stronger than the hand made brick, and cedar than sycamore, stick right up in the face they do. But Daschle speaks a curse against America when he speaks Isaiah's words. They were not a blessing, not a defense. So why does Daschle so potently identify America with Israel in its moment of Assyrian terror? Because he has a tin ear. That this tin ear keeps ticking and echoing. NY boasts it will cut a 20 ton piece of stone from the Adirondacks to use as a new cornerstone for the new Freedom Tower, later rejected. The Sycamore tree at Ground Zero that sheltered the miracle chapel is replaced by a "cedar,' a cousin pine tree. The new tower is bigger than before, raised to boasts, shaking fists, threats bravado and resolve, even to the point of continued use of language, the word defy. This puts America front and center into the bible of Isaiah 9. 10. Chapter and verse, that's where America is in the Bible. Who do they defy, al queda/ Ridiculous. you only defy some thing greater than yourself, not less. But no more than Ancient Israel does America know what it is doing when it shakes its fist.

I have good news and bad news, the harbingers of Cahn only partly apply, however the part that does is so far worse than he lets on. There has never been a more spiritless presentation of a state of emergency than Tom Daschle's snippet on the floor of the senate.

All this can be digested and rationalized as everything can if we don't look further, earlier in Isaiah. There we see much more about the cedar and the stone and fist. "For the day of Yahweh of hosts shall be upon every one that is proud and lofty, and upon every one that is lifted up and he shall be brought low. And upon all the cedars of Lebanon that are high andlifeted up...and upon every high tower...and the loftiness of man shall be bowed down...and the idols He hslall utterly abolish.. Moreover the conditions of that day are set forth for Yah-Yahweh shall "take away from Jerusalem and from Judah the stay and the staff" 3.1 that is to say the guard, the protection, the covering that had been extended over the righteous nation among many that opposed it. This shows in the destruction that follows, but more it taken away: "the might man, the warrior, judge, prophet, the prudent, the elder, the captain, the honorable, the counselor, the artist, the orator" to be replace by children: "I will give children for the princes...and the child shall behave himself proudly against the elder and the base against the honorable. The rule of law fails. Isaiah won't stop. 9 the boldness of the faces witness against them and they declare their sin as Sodom, they hide it not. That of course tears it for the modern American who is such a friend and codefendant with Sodom, but Isaiah doesn't can for "they have done evil unto themselves." When he says "children are their tyrants" he means their leadership is puerile and meaningless. check the polls. But it gets worse and worse. They "lay bare their secret parts" 4.17 not just oplympia underwear, but secret texts, mistresses, deals, leaks, lies, on and on. so that we will never be done with the effects of Isaiah before 9.10. This is called the Day of the Lord, the End times, the Last Days and America just got there in time Young says anarchy follows from poor govt I.144, but the full picture in the 9 chapters is filled out with "the mother of all threatenings 347 and the end result, "they shall eat every man of the flesh of his own arm." It's time to break out the stars and stripes.

Given the imperfect nature of our knowledge it may be more important to understand how we rationalize away what we do know rather than look for more knowing. So to understand Isaiah and 9/11, take a substiute3 parallel, James Laughlin and 9/11. It was always a scandal that America was not in the Bible. Books and sermons written about it could find no mention prophetically that America participated in the end times of *Revelations*. This was troubling to Americans because after two thousand the end times were practically the only topic of conversation. Much comfort was gained then when America, we should call it the United States, found a way to get in the Bible. Indeed Tom Dashel did it the day after 9/11, which was anyway a day much prophesied, even if the prophecies were denied. I don't mean Nostradamus, but New Directions publisher McLaughlin's planes fling in the buildings in 1948, but after the event, the next day, 9/11 began to have a transfigured existence, because it was found in the Bible, and if 9/11 was there, then behold, America was too. Good news? Yes and no. 9/11 had already had an uneven track record. Suspicions raised by architects, A&E, combined with an entire underground of surreptitious science, subverted and misreported by the press, underground trains and cities, military bases with unmentionable technologies cast doubt on the official narrative of events. But when the news becomes an archetype something beyond manipulation of facts is at hand.

You may wonder what this is about, but the bare facts include a speech and prayer George Washington made and led on April 30, 1789 convening the first full session of the new constituted government in New York city, the capital at that time. He was inaugurated at Ground Zero, now called Federal Hall Time and place are implicated in that the time was the first duly constituted nation, and place because the location of the prayer service was the same as what is known as St. Paul's chapel at ground zero. What Washington said is relevant, warning that, "smiles of Heaven can never be expected on a nation that disregards the eternal rules of order and right which Heaven itself has ordained," which seems perhaps perfunctory for the time, but by 9/11 becomes as laden with significance as some of the statements of Eisenhower about space invasion and government and business cohabitation.

The nice thing is we can leave Washington there for 212 years, says Tom Dashel, who had the honor of putting America in the Bible that many years later, because the significance of that time and place were more than doubled when the 9/11 attack coincided with both, first because the attack was against the time of that constitution at the place of the chapel. Afterward much celebration was made of the Miracle of the chapel's survival, the only building left standing around the trade center, not a window broken in the blast of the building's collapse. What saved the chapel was a tree between it and the collapse that sheltered it, a sycamore tree, but without becoming botanists a tree suffices. This tree did and did not survive. It is kept as a bronze reconstruct in the roots which hang in the center. That these roots resemble rather the spider of Bilbao would be better left unmentioned. Its stump also is preserved in form. More honor is don to this tree than to many people. The Trinity Root Today

In September 2005, a two ton bronze sculpture memorializing the surviving root of the fallen **sycamore** tree that shielded St. Paul's Chapel [Completed in 1766, it was known primarily before Sept. 11 as the place where George Washington prayed on April 30, 1789, the day he was inaugurated as president .] from debris on 9/11 was installed in the south courtyard of T…

· Installation of the Trinity Root

The root was created to memorialize the surviving root of the fallen **sycamore** tree that shielded St. Paul's Chapel, across the street from Ground Zero, from debris on 9/11.
There is also a statute of Washington at the Federal Hall now, four blocks from ground zero, so any visitor can see in embryo the point that Washington was there, but so was the destruction.

Outside the walls of information control however, the chapel speaks more of judgment that salvation, since it highlights the destruction of the 7 or so buildings surrounding

So the sycamore tree is a big deal because it preserved the chapel build in 1766 where Washington went to pray after his inaugural, where he said….Washington's speech 30 apr 1789.

Miracle of the sycamore: "*This stump is all that remains of a 100 - year-old Sycamore that once stood in the northwest corner of St. Paul's churchyard. The tree was toppled on September 11th, 2001, when the collapse of the World Trade Center sent tons of debris hurtling towards the church, including a large steel beam from the North Tower. Miraculously, the Chapel's trees shielded from dam and not a single pane of glass was broken through the church." "In 2005, renowned sculptor Steve Tobin worked with tree experts to preserve the original Sycamore stump that you see here at St. Paul's.*" (From the Plaque Below the Stump) Michael Gericke, a partner in the Pentagram studio, designed the cornerstone.

Notes:

James Laughlin (1914-1997) published many modern writers. "Above the City" first appeared in the yearly anthology of *New Directions 9* next to Henry Miller's essay on Rimbaud, "When Do Angels Cease To Resemble Themselves?" Pound told him here. See this memorial by Kenneth Patchen.

Keats and Cortez: It was really Balboa.

Nassim Nicholas Taleb: "Strangely, my book *Fooled by Randomness*, published a week before September 11, 2001, had a discussion of the possibility of a plane crashing into my office building. So I was naturally asked to show "how I had predicted the event. I didn't predict it-it was a chance occurrence" (*The Black Swan.* New York: Random House, 2007, 153-54).

John Gardner: "Beowulf looks like a fish. "*Conversations with John Gardner*. Edited by Allan Chavkin. Jackson: U of Mississippi Press. 1990, 149.

B-25: Published analysis shows that the reason the B-25 did not bring down the Empire State Building has to do with its construction and that the weight of impact was 60 to 100 times greater at the WTC. Why this did not trigger an awareness in the builders of the WTC is too much after the fact. It wasn't a mistake as much as a blind spot, an omission, a cost savings, an optimism, so even though the B-25 Bomber sounds big it was small compared to the Boeing 767 airliners, which had full fuel tanks.

Beowulf

To adjust our eyes to Polyphemus, the one eyed Cyclops (*Odyssey*, ix) as a prophet against empire, and some unknown mystery, Lucifer in Dante's image, frozen in hell (*Inferno*, xxxiv) unaware of the prophetic, immersed in imagined events, the poet does not comprehend foreknowledge. Critics *after* the predicted event identify it, but the event must first occur. Prophecies about Virgil's Fourth Eclogue and the Messianic Psalms await the birth. No one objects that Erasmus Darwin coined an "aerial steam carriage" as a precursor of the airplane or "machinery resembling the tail of a fish to be placed behind a boat" as a motor boat, though 1791 predates the actual. Who however among them gives Beowulf credit for the first submarine?

Beowulf stands before the mere without a boat. Batten the hatches. He wears a "gleaming war-corslet," a metal skin. Scales cover his body. There is a "silvery helm" on his head," "hooped with lordly bands." He is some swimmer, takes "a great part of the day" to reach the bottom of the mere. The record for holding the breath is 17 minutes 4 seconds. A current singer of the mead hall holding the breath even that long would be heroic, but the gleaming metal silvery round head piece, scales of armor make Beowulf look like a fish. John Gardner of his own *Grendel* says, "when Grendel first sees Beowulf coming, Grendel thinks of him as a sort of machine, and what comes to the reader's mind is a kind of computer, a spaceman, a complete alien, unknown. The inescapable mechanics of the universe. At other times, Beowulf looks like a fish to Grendel." Gardner: a near miss. Beowulf is a sub.

Dr. Faustus Space Program

Argonauts to such facetiousness declare without a doubt that space voyages began in Plutarch, in his Face in the Moon or in Lucian. But we take a more modern intuition of space voyage from orbiting satellites in Marlowe and Milton. Do you think it strange that the duration of orbit of both Dr. Faustus and Satan is eight days? Before his thirst for pranks and sex Dr. Faustus was so devoted to cosmology that he had wandered about the "spheres above the moon" seeking the rotation patterns of the planets. He went himself to space in a magic dragon-chariot to see the "tropics, zones, and quarters of the sky."

And whirling round with this circumference,
Within the concave compass of the pole,
From east to west his dragons swiftly glide,
And in eight days did bring him home again.

Doctor Faustus, III, 11-14

But with what diabolic mimicry does Milton's Satan run the earth to reconnoiter Eden in eight days? Dr. Faustus and Satan first in space does not exactly approbate the space program! Were infernalists first? Where the hell was Dr. Sagan? Right behind. Even if Sagan's ashes are not in space he wanted them to be. Is that why the program was canceled? Consider the eight day transit of the Milton orbiter:

The space of seven continu'd Nights he rode
With darkness, thrice the Equinoctial Line
He circl'd, four times cross'd the Car of Night
From Pole to Pole, traversing each Colure;
On the eighth return'd.

Paradise Lost, IX, 62-66

Marlowe, Milton, but who first we inquire? *Neither.* It's all from Lucian who took eight days to reach the moon. So in other words not every fiction is prophetic, especially when it imitates the classics, even Plutarch, even Lucian.

Space travel apotheosis also occurs in Blake and Shelley. Blake made all manner of such voyages. The Marriage of Heaven and Hell demonstrates the vanity of angelic "Analytics" when he kidnaps the angel and is very lucky not to collide in orbit with the unraveling Percival Lowell:

"I by force suddenly caught him in my arms, & flew westerly thro' the night, till we were elevated **above the earth's shadow**: then I flung myself with him directly into the body of the sun, here I clothed myself in white, & taking in my hand Swedenborgs volume sunk from the glorious clime, and passed all the planets till we came to Saturn, here I staid to rest & then leaped into the void, between Saturn & the **fixed stars**."

Blake's space jump has no technology yet to match so cannot be called prophetic, but remember Cassandra was not believed, and that Sophocles was 80 when he wrote *Antigone,* so from rubble civilization perhaps will think how good it once was. Anachronism is a big part of the satire opposing the prophetic. Blake kindly returns Swedenborg to his proper sphere, the stars, but facetiously, to astound the angel, for medieval cosmologies, were "*above* earth's shadow," not outside, and the pre-Copernican astronomy of "*fixed* stars," was an Empyrean beyond the seventh planet. Futurists here may think a dandy telekinesis.

But the last stanza of Shelley's celebrated *Adonais*, when Keat's "spirit's bark is driven, / Far from the shore," "borne darkly, fearfully, afar," is more apotheosis of Castor and Pollus than space launch. Shelley's sincere technology has him go "afar," but how did he get there? Nobody knows. Keats' apotheosis is classic imitation unless you think it his emergence in the ninth bardo.

So unconscious patterns embed fact. Look, up in the sky, here comes Taliesin from "the region of the summer stars!" Maybe it's the old Norman poetry, but maybe the "Hanes Taliesin" is a twelfth century space traveler! As far as we know for a fact there were none until **Shoemaker's ash** went to the moon and also that a rare piece of Tombaugh went to Pluto.

The submarine imitates a fish, the satellite a moon, rockets and airplanes birds, but the trick of consciousness limits discovery to that already found. "Canals" were discovered on Lowell's Mars and "Elysium" in America before the fact, and it's ok to imitate fish, birds or the moon, but do not talk of atomic power imitating the sun, when "it shall come to pass that at evening time it shall be light" (*Zechariah*).

Shepherd Wolf

This suggests connection of judgment with they call themselves scholars, researchers, investigators but are alarmists. The British are coming, alarmists who pose the ultimate mousetrap, but without exact decree the fates at least gave Oedipus and his fate, but things were managed better for effect in the play. In this guise the golden age was always a pretend, an extension of something that had not to do with life into life, making it a counterfeit. So if now it is said that events such as overpopulation, degradation of resources, threats of revolution will all in the end bring about a golden age that too is pretend. We have been living in the golden all our lives but knew it not. The peasant farmer lived in it, hungry and benighted as he was said to be, ignorant of the higher math, music he had, and art, and even more community. It was only when he became an individual that he began to have difficulty, that science and scholars emerged along with ever new tribal forms of society, but not like the old lived on earth under sky. If you count the number of days and nights those former ones spent in good air, under sun and star against what the modern does you see the modern is more like the putative escapees of Mars who when their living failed built a planetoid space ship as the moon Iapetus and have lived inside it ever since. That would be worse than prison shut off from the natural. The analogy holds somewhat for peoples who live in rooms and watch flickering screens, and lose their health contemplating their images in a mirror that reflect only themselves, but without the lines of age their grandparents knew.

It is to these people that the golden age appeals when they hear of it, reduced to justice, good will, fairness, peace, for these things only just disappeared in their lifetimes. Into this environment come their prophets of all kinds who think to demagogue them with facts of their own twisting, arching concepts that explain nothing but are delivered in the demagogue's style with plenty of emotion and fear, repetition and logical jumps. The new facts overwhelm people overwhelmed already by the artificial environment they find themselves in, artificial food, engineered to make they hungry and then sick. What a mistaken reality to make society sick so you can make it better again, at least in promise, for it is just made more sick with dissatisfactions so that it can never be healthy, meaning young, meaning beautiful like the models it offers in ads and runway shots and in negligees. These people, already manipulated into obesity, will believe almost anything you scare them into especially when the facts are so selected that they may be twisted into the false not the true. Give examples of this?

In the past, epics encompassed time and space in a mythic way so that events that happened long before impinged on the present along with future promises. Earth was a meeting place of the heavens, which stood for the gods mostly, who worked out their jealousies and foibles on people, but there were intrusions from the below the earth too, from the dead so to speak. Looking at this epic environment together, the one common factor on earth was that the gods wanted a girl. Zeus wanted Io, Hera was jealous, he wanted Persephone…The girls stood for life, in taking the girl they were experiencing life to its fullest, the joy of love, nothing better, no greater ecstasy or joy. The girl was everything. Get the girl and you get the gold, the gold girl was life and after than get a piece of land. These ideas came to a people immersed in earth air water and fire that they used and felt everyday. When was your last fire? The girl, the mother, the child were all subject to conquest by the man, politics, war, religion,. Why? No reason, but because they could, or did. It was for power. Because these people were not so afflicted with individualism they lived and died under the mercy that their name, family, tribe, people, way of life went on when they passed, so death was not anything except a part of life, not something to be resisted so that all the life was held hostage to it, so that while you lived you didn't live. Freed to live, work, suffer, they did so without the heroic measures science has forced upon us all. More than heroic measures, artificial fingers, liver, kidneys, hearts and toes. It was better to die to them than receive such amendments to life. Without these things they lived and died. They were let go and not suffered to remain in test tubes, beakers, dna samples, cryonic tanks to be maybe raised up with the evil of science that would contradict all that life on earth held as good from the first, life among herds with the girl, a wife, and children under sky in fields.

Science took all that away and substituted neuroses for long life without the corrective of pain, choice. You can just get a new heart, reprogram genes. Into this counterfeit age came a new epic, as if another mercy to save from all the dead artificiality of what science had made from its tubes, animal experiments and tortures it kept under wraps that even the super rich didn't know. The new epic came to restore the old life. That is why we are here today, to restore what life was by casting off the false assurances we have had that we are safe because all the lions are extinct and the wolves are on reservations and nature is not fearful. The new myths mean to restore fear so we can live existentially again, for this was forfeit in the 20th century suburbs and rights of the individual. People still go without fear to the mall. So back to ancient Israel and Greece, Babylon and Sumner and the interplay of all time and space upon the moment. It is a good thing if we rediscover our faith and that life is worth more than wealth, life is worth dying for, that life is vested with truth because there is One who made it all.

Are you saying we should be members of herds, like sheep? We were always subject to forces anyway. We are anyway except we're being sold the idea that we're not that we are individuals. Are you saying we should be Luddites and hate the present future past? The demagogues have all their news men out questioning aggressively any voice that challenges their doctrine. See, it breaks their control. We were always subject to forces so that ultimately our only choice is to live with them or die. Under the guise of false fear, read to control, they invented terrorists, but nobody's really afraid.

So what's the new myth? That **myths were never true, they were inventions to enslave.** The demagogues want to say they speak a reality like the fate that trapped Oedipus, that not only are they true, but supernaturally true, irresistibly true. True myth and false fact made a swift reversal in a decade, like they now say did the evolution of the dog. Complete control is now exercised over all thought in this captivity of continual misinformation environments.

It's not Nostradamus, or any of the other predictive associations of film.

In the War Against Imagination.

Blurb for *Grasshopper Grid:* 2nd ed Early Tattooed High Govt Habit Swine Fry Release

I admit the tree is dying.
Too much sunny aluminum today,

What you see in the mirror grid
Do not believe United.

They peck on the knot in your brain,
Ants where the woodpeckers ferret,
And black bumbles too, gold bumblebees where the peckers the
Russians are coming.

Little godlings hatch the grid,
and gophers attack the poles
scalar dynamics gone wrong and so to be changed
will be relieved if the Russians
destroy the dead conifer off *grid.*
A menagerie of *woodpeckers*
Woodpeckers and dudder physics,
simulations, mop up the slabs.

In this 2nd ed release of early tattooed high govt art
That inhabits the *Grasshopper* swine flu fry brain,
Trigger gibber code record a **hyno**-gram courier
toolbox, microwaves, stolen
gravity down from hypothemes,
Freedom of Thought Information lies
piece by piece, nouns and verbs cut off.
post, recall, go blank, go left, go right.
Did it rain? Do you remember the command?

Electric erasure got the flu,
psycho science signaled now.
Project X ten Thousand codes,
Eureka replaced Mind Control.
Hypno- NLP defense
Eureka pleasure center, sales technique.

In the war against imagination
George Romney,

Jack Ruby,
National Security,
Dept of Energy,
General Atomics,
fusion orbit,
spider web satellite tech,
quarantined pygmy speech
red herring tech.
Fake Grey abduction,
stun gun amnesia tech,
Screen scrambles,
ritual deficit disorder,
MPD military hypno-courier.
Delta Force Waco trigger verse,
dissociate and look.

Janet Reno and Anthony Robbins
Had a mind brainwash Sirhan rapport,
Elsberg, Leary cryptocrat,
presidential model hypnosis
Ear receivers, ping pong eyes,
mad scientist white sound
drum and fire ever cease to civ.
All news, station Crypotech,
Carl Nicholi, NSA stunt,
repeal the Act. Inalienable right,
2nd ed release tattooed
high govt swine fry flu.

Epstein's Chomsky Charlie Wittgenstein & Whorf

Now that gas and teeth compel

the bridge of nunca mas,

e-Ghibboleth religion politics

Follow the facts! Follow D51.

You say you don't believe

A fundamental boundary sets the stage!

A 9self formulated crypto id

clones

those who decay!

Want to know what cometh next?

Pipe organs grown in pigs.

Start with the treasure in their stones!

Remade dinosaurs of all kinds $cience led,

but ?usiness was behind.

Super soldiers mounted schnitzels pulled by legs.

Godzilla and the monsters Pop,
in bed we know with nanobots,
Dinosaurs sought better fate

a 50ah's flood of shrinking spherical shapes.

All purists on the goof coasts wrote
of Thunder Dawn and corkscrewed rope.
Houston Island planted hemp, grafted Oak & Pine
In one hand iron gripped their brain

Visions of Providence,

Shakalo Urijah, Micah one
plunging the waves of Toledo, Akron done.
Miami, Nulon Rouge.

They wrote Star pot Pashur, cartilaginous John,
Jonah, Ismael and Basha vermilion.

Because we dared to reach the hearts
Of that Great Britain west,
Akron for Gaza was mistaken,
Manhattan desolate drove out day.
L.A. saw the global shaken out to tread the clay.

Tread mortar down, make brick strong,
The Queen is stripped and led away.
Tertius Orbis Flash wakes up,
Fictionauts grave imaginate IED He-il.
Light and shock more felt than sought
disinfect the wind wake up.

Again the bone boats sail.

Japan went sleeping to the sun
Straight out Forces shot to hide the light
of blindness, disorient fish.
To light the blind Rowboats loaded pennies
pushed beyond the lunar mount.

Prepare for Super Bill's Adorn the millennial
underground
Diverted, meaning Superflat, the hawking god,
Godzilla worked beside.

Get down, get down comprachicoes,
took Valium and Lust & disinfectant drugs
to build the pleasure state.

Spontaneous precog analogues,
which Palsy took in Rage,

pharmacopoeia New transcendent

was the dawn of the age.

Johnny Cake

You remember Syn? **Syn** was lost but Pancake rescued her from Dragon. Joe Pan flew down in his marvel wave machine and killed the bad and returned her home nice to mom. “Get hold of them electric lights and make ads.” Nothing Christmas cannot be changed to its opposite!

"In the smelter the solid runs." Recase the solid unsolid god of the age, **ePANCAKE!**
Good to eat and good for you each morning.

Making way for telecom products, retribed monkeys, themselves virtually human, needs no labels or lapels to buttonhole. Ordain the identification. It's the difference between tomato and nut. The think glands are walnuts.
Weverboy's walking around with nuts inside.
He get too big we shrink'em.
Too small we give supplements.
Jo Pan spoke the eloquent marvels of podcasting the familiar to the divine. "You can do it too," he urged the mannequin children who worked through the boxed syntax of Syntazz.

Rip Law was another character in the Pancake Empire. In later T shirts he escaped and had a black mask, oh Ignatius!
His schemes were manifold. Not that they touched flesh that ate raw food or played among the rocks tracking lizards, followed bee lines to water or stalked deer in a friendly manner. That's how to learn to hunt, to hunt. To be still, be silent. To be invisible, what won't come to such a one!

So **Johnny Cake** ran.
Outran every other.
Johnny Cake was Pan Cake
who was like Rip Law
who was like igod
and he ran and ran and he ran.

He got himself out of oven town.
He got himself up-pulled, fup, by his straps.
He could have been American.
He won a gold medal.
It was just that simple.

He said, "I think I can." He out ran his brother, his parents, the work doers, the wolf and the bear, but the **fox**, that lousy fox waited.
"Here is a world where everybody is disproving themselves," that was **Flesh**'s discovery of the spirit world. The spirit world was the physical world inhabited by the people opposed to the physical world inhabited by animals and plants.
Things make sense if you turn them upside down.

People were carrying around the spirit inside and it was spoiling the outside. Physically they were good red meat and blood and bone and that could easily go thump, thump.

And that was all right. Like animals.
But spiritually it was another patchin -- stuffed with rags and cotton and had shoe button eyes, which is why they couldn't see the sequence of action. Little rag heads thought they were in a soda water ghetto afraid of being made into soup, all soft and loppy and full of cotton and not empty at all or hollow like someone had said.

Course what is cotton but filler and you could as easy use corn shucks or stuffing, straw man or batting, just anything to fill a void.
So spiritually they really didn't work and needed fill.
Stuffed stuffing and wadding and packing and when you unwrapped the shell there was nothing in it at all but packing.
The only explanation anybody gave for this was that they fell through a hole or what and ended up here in this land. That was the extent of their spiritual wasold.
Universally there used to be an outside and an in, an up and down, now there was only an in. The kingdom heaved on the banks but without there was faeries and boloins, fiction and faction.

"The great still pressed bird song and orange count cobbled to a hoax."
If you're flesh out to save the button you care about such.

Thee was not.
Thee didn't mean to do it.
Thee was pushed.
That evil had about decided thee wasn't much since thee never did nanny thing that it could see. This vastly opaque style of life.

There is no time to go into what it consists of, but evil could see into the little ragherds since it had also planned the rag hearts.
"Yes take for granted that there are **spiritual organs**, counterparts to the physical, some more notable than others. The spirit liver. The circumcision of the heart."

What does our flesh do with that?
Male vestiges of feminine spirit.
Reflections through a dark flask.

Have ever yourselves a peek of the naked heart, or will'ya leave it in the **pericard**, hangin' on the rack sweet? The heart reclothed in a T- shirt with a slogan blessed.
Once circumcised fears the fire better.
Hide, hide it don't you think? The truth is exposed .
Clothe the heart?

"The shadow of the might" said Pearl. It will cover me with fathers. Cut then cover. Cut the fat, cut the sweet. Purify by blood not work.

"Who is your tailor?"
I buy the rack.
There is a grain of camphor for the poor in the notion that the first shall be last. Look what happened to Lazarus. Somewhere exist the idea of just. But they say God looks on the heart.
The post delivers mostly bills, junk mail and only once a year that check.

"Shall I do evil that good may come?"
That is the flesh question, thinking of the cowman to murder.
"But did not the Aposty say he wished himself cursed for the people, poetically quoting those who ask to be a killed in place of the people?"
The pleoplle always the poeop-ple, take all evil upon him that good may come. Specious thoughts. The serpent as the most subtile beast virtually formed the native plant society for his own purposes. Preserve the Prairie. What org not infiltrated with cunning?
The good was evil the evil was good.
The cow and its could.
The boy in the hood.

Dead meat of food.
Is a burger spiritual outside the meat?
To such uses high mind is put.
Hunt a really good spiritual
smell of earth burger.
A cockcrow bourger.
No chicken patty slice of pungent air,
a burger that will satisfy till tummy rocks and gobbets of
sun sprinkle alchemy dawn. Swell tin place.
A brink of a burger spiritually speak.
The bourgner the burgher, the burfger, the buffgeefer
meat.
I told you spirit worlds ruin the physical!
What to do?
The kingdom's within all the machinations of man
continual.
But the evil is good. Good economy. Good evolution.
Good psychology. Without evil. Boring. So be glad the
evilisgood. What did you expect. Whow could he do it to
me? Assuming he did. Picking the wings off flies.
Daming the Grand Canyon. Rototiling the ear.
"Why he do it?"
"What the charge?"
"You did yourself you bleeding nainny!" Anything can
be turned opposite. Ever yourselves peek at the naked
heart?

"And could he be the boy next door?" No, it is the sprit of lawlessness next door. What else can you say of them when they don't rake or plow their lawn or even if they do?

Man make up your mind. Spirit or flesh?

"What If the end comes and I don't feel like it?"

He upulled himsle fup by his own boot straps.

He could dhave been amermican.

He won a gold medal.

It was just that silmple. He sadi "I thilnk I can, I knew I could."

He outsran his mbrother, hils parents, the workders, the woldf and the fbear

but **fowx** was wailting.

Magical Sicario

We have to believe the magical because it explains the loss of all reason in the lives of those we know, rather like the obfuscating and editing staff intelligence to policy makers to gaslight the truth, whether fathers or governments, since fathers are governments, stronger with forbearance, not swept away by the magical negative state.

To comfort this murder city dreamland of the *sicario* of Charles Bowden's teeth worn invisibly around his neck and now thrown in the soup, Magical Thinking is one of two ways to be safe and sane, but requires silence, which means pretend nothing is happening. Facsimiles refuse to say out loud the images of our torture and suffering, saving the best for second best, magical thinking: "inventing various explanations for what you refuse to say and by these explanations dismiss the very thing you cannot let pass your lips" (35). Psychopaths pretend to be fairy princesses because as innocents they were made to masturbate their priest, cop, teacher, and worse. They maintain silence. To speak the horror is horror. Truth cannot pass their lips. It would result in the destruction of life as they know it. But pretend sublimation is subjugation.

If city is a narcotecture, magical thinking is a psychotecture supported by the dream amnesia of TV, radio, and didg. These are the sweet drugs of fantasy (61). Truth's sacrifice, as everyone knows, supports the pretend civilization and its tortured life. Truly you will be torn limb from limb:

"There is recourse to Magic if things are not said, then these things do not exist. Just as some people cleanse their vocabularies of racial slurs or sexist terms and, by that act, convince themselves they are altering reality and ending tribal or religious or racial strife and bring men and women into some kind of purity and joy, so *there is a magical belief that to ignore the killings, to deny the violence, to refuse to admit to fear, these decisions lower the temperature of human rage or human mayhem or erase fear or the things to fear.* It is a form of prayer practiced without a church" (78, emphasis added).

I'm just trying to get his books out of the house and go back to watching *Macbeth,* otherwise avoid becoming the cadaver dog at ground zero who "sat down on the rubble...and never worked again. Apparently, the magnitude of the scents overwhelmed his soul" (Dreamland, 72). Bowden explains the impossible. To me there is no knowing except to dash them in pieces. When Spanish Cortéz met the native, or iron met obsidian, as Bowden says (probably stole it from Galeano), that Sword would rend the civilized heaven, meaning "the moment when iron met obsidian and obsidian offered up its women" (105).

How there can be such a harvest that artists and poets not wonder? How in less than 100 years could earth tripppple its population! Bowden says the city itself is a factory where "new human beings in quantities far greater than the market can absorb cut babies with giant machines from templates of mind. Every year production quotas are raised and more redundant human beings are fabricated and cast out into the streets." (Dreamland, 25).

Magical Compartments

So "nothing in his appearance signals what he has been and what he has done." What assassin, that's the governor! Stay inside when these bubbles blow. You can add the rosy dawn of Cialis to make the greatest nation of the earth! And when the iron room...what iron room? When the air leaves the iron room...on TV, to neuter and strengthen the bloom...not done? Not Yet!

It is a comfort to read *The Revelation*. But again, the "purpose of this book is not to answer the reader's questions but to teach the reader a new reality, one in which an American reader's normal questions are absurd because the reader has entered a world of terror and total corruption" (*El Sicario*, xiii) which is broader and braver than that, but do not ask what is it. There is a coming visit. New reality! Hardly are those words out when spiritus mundi bubbles in front. Two for one, Prufrock and Yeats, nice. I think the two are one, Yeats scuttling, to find his grave. Did you know he had a substitute? I guess not. They don't teach the new reality. It must be kept, a nice magical under Ben Bulben, "for example, if you are assigned to kidnap someone, then you deliver the victim to another person, El Dos, who delivers him to El Tres, who will deliver him to the person who executes him, who then delivers him to the person who buries the body" (79)?

Lord knows I don't care where they bury the body, but you know the end. In our case, to brainwash, it will be assumed conform to the grant. 90% of physics majors paid by government, offered NDEA grants to study linguistics—key to the eye hole, to the brain hole, heart hole, holey mole--DARPAOLE. Look ordinary (viii) but be sompin else. El Dos TV Net to eat, El Tres dress them nice, consumption is complete, which Cuatro will electromagnetically make. FEMA cometh, and then the coup de grace. Seven Billion bodies gonna live with God.

Magical Disappearance

Don't believe it. Iron, iron on the wall. These rhymes are solid as youtube, called the los levantados, not raptured, kidnapped. And the iron wall, you can't just drive around, but built "into this wall are gates that will allow armored trucks to pass through" (*Murder City*, 188). It is arranged. Plato o Plomo? Silver or lead? My Bowden asks, "what do you do when the whole country is invaded, infiltrated completely" (171). What do you do when the tow truck stops at your door? The answer heretofore has been you will not know it is a tow truck. You'll think magically it is an ice cream truck. So be a good sport as the mothers of Juarez are saying, paint the telephone poles pink and cover them with black crosses. Find your maquilas.

Blood Orchid. An Unusual History of America

Begin the Bowdeen

Just when you think Bowdeen has gone off the rails to the Seminary of the Damned you realize he is talking about the history of the unthinkable from Ancient Mayan to Argentina to Vietnam. Of ten million natives dead of smallpox and a hundred million buffalo removed. You try to put that up and get a bad connection. How can his genre be called nonfiction when in the midst of charging the gold statue of sacrifice they are running the corridors of the Pentagon to retrieve their files, the farmers from Hanford, Washington with their gold tumors, the one breasted women from Utah, uranium miners wheezing, squads of wolves and mountain lions to discover what happened to the forests, glowing radioactive tortoises, mobs of shoeless Mexicans, dolphins and orcas with embedded radio collars each lunging for their files where their lives are buried alive? He brings those responsible to the bar. Run by Uncle of course, so-called, and Christopher Hitchens of Oxford, Harvard men also, graduates bludgeon into consciousness the minds of the sodden. Read all in reverse. Bowdeen takes us to where flesh and blood scent moral outage. Liberals and puritans in the seminary of hell? This public service brought to you, hosed in paragraphs over tourists in writing.

The only difference between Bowden exposing the MX test sites, the folders of the Cabez Prietra gunnery ranges, the killings of the wastelands and the hundreds of websites on everything from the poles of Saturn to the depths of the Denver Airport are that millions read and believe those, but only hundreds read Bowden and believe or care. Even if he is one of those post-human voices you hear for the last time: "I step over a dead secretary—her head apparently severed by a now serene one-breasted woman who is resting in an ergonomically designed chair—and walk down the corridor with the file" (229). No wonder there is gunfire and murder, prostitution and drug dealing throughout, it is all that is left. "We have all we need—except, ah except, we have no beliefs" (230). He shows it for what it is, no different from Micah flying over those "who also eat the flesh of My People, and flay their skin from them; and they break their bones, and chop them in pieces, as for the pot, and as flesh within the caldron" (3). The only ones who don't want Bowdeen to sound the Bible are all the scientists, all of the secularists and all of the rest. But what goes around comes: "you shall not have a vision and it shall be dark to you that you shall not divine, and the sun shall go down on the prophets and the day shall be dark over head."

If you want to be a prophet, be a loner; a writer, be a brooder. Nobody knows the progress of the migrante like Chuck. It is the burden of Arizona to the barren, Bowden and Abby, not Goldwater, McCain and Keating, not the Mormons of Snowflake, the bears and elk of the White, pasture of wilderness, the rock sky. Get to the concrete, but you won't like it, cruelty of the milkweed human. Prophecy in the end is always about the human and what it means.

It must be a gift to excite such rancor and contempt in people half your age to judge you by their callow ways as they do the war torn Bowden, who don't want to hear the prophet, "the two groups I know who are most alike are environmentalists and pornographers," (95) pious and subpious as grammarians. The oldsters pay him no mind, don't read him at all. "I feel like I am escaping from a crypt." (92) Bowden is a lost Christopher Hitchens without a creed or a Way or junk energy from cigarettes and booze enough to kill him, it takes a dope, a revolutionary '68 whose revolt failed when the parakeet in the cage died, and then... "what went wrong with my life, my country, and my times?" (xv)

Bowden and Bowdeen

Looking for hopelessness in a hopeful world he finds Loren Eiseley's Star Thrower fin de siecle homily, "the last land tortoise had fallen victim to the new expressway. None of his kind any longer came to replace him. (78, 89). Bowdeen wants apocalypse, wants to "piss into the fires of hell" but Heracles turned the rivers to clean his mess, not that Bowden hasn't been to desert or river, but that's why I like him, me for whom miracles happen and the tortoises amble down the street of our town looking for a mate. I ask Big Guy, all full grown and clean as glass of milk,—

"WE'VE BEEN IN A LONG WAR AND WE'VE LOST THAT WAR AND THE WAR HAS POISONED US AND OUR GROUND...IF WE ADMIT THESE FACTS, WE MIGHT BE ABLE TO SURVIVE. IF WE DON'T, IT REALLY WON'T MATTER BECAUSE WE WILL BE FUNCTIONALLY DEAD." (xvi) — What, do you think your ideas even make sense to yourself?

I have the only full grown momma tortoise on at least the block, so bring him in, and he has lived so since, not in her arms when the small rain down Would rain, but near her den. Today he is following her, bobbing up and down and there is funny business of the 20 and the 70. This is to say if you don't like Bowdeen you must be too serious a sinner and should lighten up, for "we were too happy with the raw liver smeared against our lips to worry about the vanishing hoof prints" (5)

THE BLOOD ORCHID IS THE ATOMIC BOMB, the greed, the labor of thousands in its making, the belief in government, the killing of the buffalo by the ten millions until the orchids turn from fibrous roots into cables of our being "the roots getting thicker by the year, the first fine lines like lace on the bark of our lives...then coarsening as more and more wealth and power and energy surges through [a living gasoline explosion-Dario] and at first the roots begin to look like snakes, then like cables and later like giant aqueducts, the hidden heart pounding to the beat of explosives." (8) **But in its truest essence the blood orchid is a metaphor of the post-human, which in short is the replacement of humanity by artificial intelligence.** Granted, when "biological" this hardly seems artificial, but it is the ultimately conscienceless pretense even while it assumes the moral high ground of its own self arrogation. So whether we speak of social networks or hybrid life forms all are ultimate goods to benefit the human, understanding that as the post-human. How does it feel to be one of the beautiful people? As Leonard Cohen says, all the important mass murderers listened to the Beatles. These destructions and extinctions Bowdeen witnesses are but tangled weaves and counter weaves of DARPA, to call it by just one arm of its tentacles.

That's why we have lost the war. Get over it! But the blooms of the blood orchids, image of America and its ways, are more fearsome, all consuming old and young, a narcotic unresisted, but as he says later of the Indian, maybe the hundred year drunk, our high, was the only way the old ways could have survived, for they were not assimilated, they were drunk and rejected and all the efforts to acclimatize their language away failed-because they were drunk. "They say the blood orchids cannot be removed, they say we have grown dependent upon them" (12)...for centuries people have faced manifestations of the blood orchids, they have seen strange clouds, felt something seize their bodies they did not fully understand, died painful and surprising deaths. Felt the heel on their necks. And not given in or up." (14) So by the metaphor you know that maybe the survival of humanity is a drug-drunk century necessitated while the machines take over. Would it were so to have mastered the art of the anesthetic. Bowden perfectly predicts, blindly, the arrival of H+, "We had to kill the thing we love [ourselves, Humanity] to prove our love...We had to sacrifice our women to prove our love—so many one-breasted ones now ambling around as testimony to our adoration. Kill the thing we love. That is our central legend" (15).

The mutilation of earth, the mutilation of woman, the mutilation of health, nobody can say why fish have sores in the gulf, autism rates rocket, rocket is our favority epithet, it all rockets, everything but the GNP, that rocket fell to earth, I knew not where so I made a list of it here, called it Pray It Not Strange, add to it often, links, back links, vids, arts... Potheads among the gold, "We have achieved our Historical Absolute like good Doktor Hegel promised us so long ago. We have made our entire nation into a reservation" (17).

How to tell the minor prophets from the major, the body of work, the lyricism, the suffering. "And at the end of the rainbow, by God, there is pot" (18). He says pot but we read all the other emollients, dilutions of our six minds right up to the point where we believe we are no longer valuable or even that we are what we are. Pot like rockets. "We have the best orchid garden on the surface of the earth." If you're a major prophet they divide you into thirds. There is no deutero Amos. Isaiah was sawed in two. It remains to saw in two the minor Bowden. "I now think that things are occurring so far beneath the daily patter of our civilization that we can both feel the tremors and at the same time ignore them. I think we are dying, and what we are dying from is from what we are" (85) "I am a provincial. I am incapable of sacrifice. I need to violate myself" (99, 100). If you can't see it yourself, the culture of death, then see it in him, in Bowden, "I feel I am with the dead" (101) I can now look for a miracle." (102)

All you need to be a prophet is the truth. Truth, inherently prophetic, shattering, "because Ephraim made altars to sin, altars shall be his sin" Hosea. Is there iniquity in Gilead? they sacrifice bullocks in Gilgal. "The sacrificers of men who made idols of their own understanding kiss the calves."

One thing you have to admire about Chuck, he lives in the midst where we all of us be dead, like Johan flailing up on the beach, Jonah, but I think he is Johan with a second breath, the two halves of Isaiah coming together in the resurrection, the three boys dancing in the furnace, these things go on and on. Among the prophets axeheads float and angels breathe in the face of Sennacherib. "I cannot tell if I am waiting for someone to kill me or waiting for someone to turn on the lights." (126) Bribed to say these things, to laud the unlaud, the details, dust, people, the story, the escritoires, each idol crushed.

Prophecy isn't in words it's in tropes, mystery plays and silent allegories, examples of being. He is a prophet in this sense, not a saint. He bears in his own body and mind the marks of our depravity and defeat at forces bigger than ourselves, not just sex and commercialism but greed and fear, those two most bestial nodes. "I believe in the instant we forget we commit a sin" (110) He is a prophet like Hosea who marries a whore to mirror the unfaithful, like Ezekiel who ate dung, like Elecuria who says the poor are all prophets who mirror our poverty for us so no wonder we hate them and mistreat them. He is a prophet the way woman abused is prophetic of the earth abused everywhere. It is useful to know these people are even on the planet.

"In that day one shall take up a parable against you with a doleful lamentation and say We be utterly spoiled."

Om Chomsky

Looking pole to pole, discovering what one would never want to know, a gravity of landscape, language and incomprehensibility where collective moths lament their mythlessness, I ride the subway watching natives chew on their arms. Blood dripping down the pants leg, I see on freeways shrouded in mist, or dust, to be literal. People who believe nothing is a nature in itself cannot see them chewing on their arms. I think I am angry about it, but it hurts my observations. They think their arms are pencils.

What Baudelaire said of Goya is true of Brueghel: "Goya's great merit consists of making the monstrous plausible. His monsters were born viable. Nobody has managed to surpass him for a sense of the possible absurd. All these contortions, these bestial faces, these diabolical grimaces are pierced with humanity."

Detail of Bruegel's painting The Fall of the Rebel Angels

"Pieter Bruegel the Elder's painting The Fall of the Rebel Angels shows us there really is a force to subtraction: you subtract from an angel until you end up with a demon. If you download an image of the painting onto your computer, or better yet see it hanging in the Royal Museum of Arts in Antwerp, you will notice how the rebel angels fall from heaven at the top left of the canvas to hell at the bottom right. Their wings are at first subtracted for the lesser wings of bats and dragons. Towards the earth they are reduced to moths, frogs and other soft things. They are driven together by the golden angels of heaven armed with effulgent discs, lances and swords, whose task it is to sanitise our world. You will see how the rebel angels continue to change their forms as they are driven into a sea, whose opening is an obscure drainpipe. They lose their legs, wings, all hope of surfacing, and become fish, squid, spawn and seeds of trees never to be planted.

Underwater they continue to be subtracted from their former selves until they are at last incorporeal and see-through at the bottom."

The different relation of natural and spiritual in this parallels our holidays, customs and language. Astronaut-anthropologists plummet the depths, but overlook the backgrounds of our world in theirs.

They like psychological disfigurement in this world, remove the memory of dislocated joints with a stultifying powder, an anesthetic escape. The mind cannot recall its stunting of the spine, burning the face, the incisions, manipulations, restraints. The drug deadens, and if remembered, the anesthetic masks the pain. While Consciousness reconstructs by removing the bandage, the pain of realization of a lifetime is denied by professionals. Trauma and consequent memory pose a dilemma. Without memory they could have gone mutilating forever, that is when it is not on stage performing as art and science.

It's certainly too much to believe public events are staged when one hardly believes commercials are. Evidence is only necessary because careerists in the news find themselves marginalized if they say so. That iridescent shine in the eye of the model who takes the drug is airbrushed. Events are staged so much we read them as real, hardly believe greater events are made to drive sympathy or anger, manipulate minds of masses.

That the greater whole still needs manipulating is a comfort. The job is incomplete. It's end however is dark. A clue comes for a moment because we have been thrown out of the circle by some chance. The mind skips and we see differently for a second.

Boxcars, Airports, Spaceships and Other

This Ararat Art as divination of the unconscious is as risky as the difference between reality and film, as anybody can see in the EU parliament and Breugels, or in the Guggenheim and Denver. The FEMA train beast, animated from within, now filled with paper, originally carried cargo manacled end to end. The guillotine was added by later designers as a projection, so overcome were they of a means to liquidate 15 million. There must have been a market for blood, rocketing down the night tracks hermetically sealed, no cracks in the floors like the Nazi boxcars had. Weissmandel, rabbi of Slovenia, cut with a dull blade through the bottom of that boxcar entering Auschwitz and escaped like our Lockerbie.

It is necessary to distinguish two governments at least, but the government Underground did not use Lockerbie's escape as reason to forgo the home market of guillotine use. Who would not want a guillotine in the closet, they argued, where, when it is not performing its design, a stray rooster could be dealt with, or for cutting cheese, eggs, bread and meat? Not as if any of this was new to Pol Pot, Stalin, Franco. It's a lot redundant, but all who join the guillotine throng could assume the honor with Sir Thomas More at the hip, even if his head is not yet on the battlement, or be a subject for Madame Tussaud.

"A home is not complete without. In religion they formed Assuaged Care Incorporate as the shrine of Moloch at hospital beds. Millions and millions of human stem cell donors gave up their genes, or had them expropriated, which fulfilled the double need of assuaging guilt and stocking labs. Animals, humans, plants and earth were sated with the illuminate. Idols in every grocery sang, "come buy, come and buy," The idols are on TV!" As you can see Lockerbie is a bit of a poet.

"To say this was the product of the gods disbelieved, contradicts. To say that One rules and many contradicts illustrates why the System machine could not think H like. We are living contradictions, no matter what its power. To be or not to be, our constant doubt, faith, belief, unbelief, peace, war. It's not we are opposite, but contradictorily so. Anyway, if the machine cannot program it to program itself not, out of existence, it cannot be us. We presume this good. Law, break law, teleologic suspend, natural law as well. This was the scandal of science, that truth should break law, but we gave that right only to ourselves. One works to perfectly communicate the essence of contradictory man. No matter. *Remember contradiction well. If none, know you are machined!*"

3. Photographing the FEMA Boxcar

"Books of martyrs are full of stuff that happens in those train yards, "after you worship Saturn you make a portable Moloch to carry around its gods." This Saturn seemed both train and beast. It sounds like B. Traven and that reckless *Boxcar Named Desire.* The gods had their counterpart among men and government to show how wonderful when they work combined! Among those expendable containers of population reduction and higher consciousness-gathered levels of information in *Fusion Centers*, that wrecked boxcar showed evidence also of two hundred million plastic grave liners, when only 50 million were needed. One could hold at least four. How's that for government waste? How will they

die? That's being prepared, as every martyr from Rome and before could hope for, population reduction being a must, which proves that FEMA camps do not exist on Archuleta Mesa, Greenbrier (VIP only) and a hundred plus sites. Neither is there evidence for the 129 Deep Underground Military Bases (DUMB) Schneider found in Kansas and Nebraska nor the *Ten Sectors* that house the *Underground Cities* below the *Residential Centers* above. And if there were it would only be to keep you safe. Neither are these fantasy underground cities staffed with alien and international soldiers. A lot of this material generates from a lecture by Phil Schneider of May 1995, Underground Bases financed by trillions yearly in black budgets."

"As to the involvement of Orion, Sirius or them alien buggers in earth, who you gonna believe? Philer says Eisenhower's Treaty of 1954 allowed experimentation of "implantation techniques" on humans in exchange for all this technology [interview with Schneider's wife here]. So now we know how Steve Jobs got his Apple, important because it wonderfully elaborates the Mandarin conundrum where the gods give power and control in exchange for one human life to torture forever, (code for adrenal glands and get high). Why don't they just synthesize? The muse is silent on that, but another caveat, courtesy of Schneider, holds true even as the Sky Station Senators stand at the airport, raising their middle fingers in welcome (which we're not supposed to be saying by the way, even if

you're hoping it's Denver). Different teams at different times display on alternate Thursdays."

"If Schreiber is credited they should not point up but down. He got in the worst trouble of his life at that Archuleta high plateau when rappelling down the cavern. His wife said, "he peed in his hard hat and threw the pee at the aliens which killed some of them. Many years later I would see a fictional program on TV where aliens were highly allergic to ammonia and would die from it" (here)."

"Ill equipped as we are for space flight it is heartening to think that we may yet defend the planet at our feet with the time honored Ed Abbey Defense. He, on first sighting the Grand Canyon: "the first thing I did was urinate off the rim onto a little aspen" [*One Life at a Time Please*, 124]. Research has proved that what is welcome to an aspen is noxious to a grey alder. Beyond the power of uric acid and its weaponization, the question is whether distance in time and space matter in suffering to a human onlooker is still worth pursuing. Does one feel implicated in the fate of another? That is, shall the Chinese Mandarin be executed with impunity by the European for some putative good, merely for the exercise of power, or is that repugnant?"

"Whether this is a nightmare out of Nazi science where there is no end of sacrifice of the foreigner, the alien, the Mandarin, even those of one's own party if

disenfranchised, it is all for the good of the party in power, established controls. But there is no sense of utilitarianism in the choice, no good for the greatest number. There is good for those in power! Since these boxcars and their adjuncts are to claimed 5/6 to 7/8 of humans by 2029, I'm not sure who's reading this. That fate is better though than the passenger pigeon, but not to take lightly. There were 100,000 missing milk carton children and 550,000 missing children on the FBI report for 2011. As Denver Mural 2 notes, this is insignificant in comparison with The Greada Treaty which bought all this technology."

"Cosigners of the GREADA TREATY did not keep their word. Proponents in Cosmic Court argued that since the Great White Father didn't what's to say they should? After promising to turn in lists of humans kidnapped and tortured, glands and brain cells, six or seven million turned up missing. Then they began taking illegal aliens. Immigration didn't exactly make you Like Ike. You'd have thought he knew better being a general of the Milt-Ind Comp. A bromide sold? Ike and his mere paper against the Military Industrial Complex sold the rest of us. Our comfort was the Manacled Railway Cars, which Nazis made, but obsolete. US Steel in its place made better seats for the better life designed for them who knew. You'd think some conspiracy afoot. You'd think a vast image out of spiritual mundi covered my sight. At least the Gunderson cars had side vents! In consideration of all this a silver lining is due. The

manufacture of Manacled Railway Cars revived the boxcar industry from near extinction by cargo trains. Big Steel made seats for fifteen million to be hauled to a better life, over 100,000 boxcars in all, good for the economy and good for share holders!"

I don't know if you're still with us in this Report, but you might know that once a Psychiatrist gets going they don't easily stop. I tried to tell him there was a tomorrow, but he interrupted me with this:

"You conspiracy people need to get a life, count on that. Even if wind socks are blowing inside double stranded barbed wire fences along railroad tracks from Van Horn to Marfa, it makes a very very very fine house, a childrens' playground with two cats in the yard, but it has no airport! [you are meant to play these songs as you read!] Has Halliburton got to do everything? Denver Airport too? No wonder Anubis is on guard. Execution orders are executive orders, enemy POW camps are residential centers, biological pandemics give no excuse. I won't give the House bill numbers in case of civil unrest. *With higher consciousness comes higher crime.* Ain't it wonderful when gods and men work together! Nor should one quibble when millions and millions have gone before, given a back to the smitters and cheeks to them that pluck hair. Whatever the outcome, whatever justice outcries rise from blood, we run toward it singing. Look at the installation of the thousand melting men, the 2501 Migrantes, the mass nudes, the tortures of

***The Fixer*, Solzhenitsyn, Guernica, Goya, George Pratt, Find Me A Voice, Paul Ruiz and Stay off the Jersey Turnpike. Now hit the gas!"**

"Preserving the brains of geniuses was a new phenomenon starting with the brain of German mathematician Carl Friedrich Gauss a hundred years before. His brain was studied by Rudolf Wagner. Its weight was 1,492 grams and the cerebral area equal to 219,588 square centimeters. Also found were highly developed convolutions, suggestions of genius (Dunnington, 1927). Other famous brains removed and studied include that of Vladimir Lenin [1340 grams] and the Native American, Ishi. The brain of Edward H. Rulloff, philologist and "criminal of superior intelligence," was taken after his death in 1871; in 1972, it was still the second largest brain on record (New York Times, Nov. 7, 1972, p. 37)." Anatole France [970 grams!] see here

[I too wonder if the guillotine wasn't added embellish. Rocketing down the tracks, hermetically sealed, shiploads of Chinese guillotines to enforce the Noahide laws sound just entertaining enough to believe when the constitution is suspended is a subject of Madame Tussaud: "Tussaud!" the Musical, would be a posthumous installment.]

III. "You understand that all these things first happened in the asylum where the Neptune forces provided a list of Blow Ups to restore the gods: Anectine, Benzedrine, bufotenine, bulbocapnine, cocaine/Demerol, dihydro-oxy-heroin, harmine, LSD6, mescaline, muscarine, scopolamine (Benway, *Naked Lunch*), *Changa!* Stood in for the thousands of instant drugs of Change! Change was the melting pot from the many to the Global One."

Naturally we wanted to know how the Heads did their work. Dr. Franke said that poets who argued, "everything is holy," also said it was a crime to shrink a god, meaning themselves. Poets being their own pushers. Nobody took more drugs. Ginsburg played his tambourine and sang "smoke dope, smoke dope." Supposedly only PK Dick said, "Don't Smoke. Don't Smoke!" Don't ask, Franke said, "Let's do the time warp again!" Blow'em back up!"

As the Neptune forces invented more and more Heads there were continuous programs on every station: peace and happiness for every man! [*Karma*, 7:19-8:50]. Peace and happiness got all jazzed. When Franke achieved Contact! he said, "For sure you can be a godling too, knowing good and evil dude!" Which is where they open the ball.

After *Contact* Dr. B said the pronouncement would come that earth was free, which the poets had sung, even if the engineering was still incomplete.

What with the ethos of every nation *made* Modern all these geographical entities could be gone. "It's a be just like Rome!" Franke's sidekick, Campbell-Joseph trotted out the chorus of mystery meth, "Break out!" And that's when Franke said: "We on the planet dog," and he burped like a frog. Just so you know, the rapping kept a person busy.

He went back and forth in these tirades, sometimes like a patient, sometimes like a scientist."It's like an interplanetary war. The weapons are programming with drugs. Anectine therapy conducted on non-volunteer inmates." But against all reason, while Franke told what he had done, a sense of outrage emerged in his voice, as if he had suddenly sprung a conscience.

Under covert guidance anectine stops the breathing so the "subject" feels like they are dying. It is a chemical variety of water torture. The attendant keeps them breathing with a machine. As the involuntary muscles collapse they are told, "this is what will happen if you *break the law*." Law means program conditioning, just before subject loses consciousness. Then the respirator is turned back on and the "subject" is brought back from the death. Life and death, life and death. They did Khalid Sheikh Mohammed 180 times, but that was with

plain water. This could work in a hundred social programs where the Monarch with its antennae removed shatters its psyche into many. Then the many are turned back into the one control. (Butterflies Use Antenna GPS to Guide Migration).

"Macro alters too large to understand and personal alters referenced too small, are practically invisible. Macros occupy a drawer with many folders. It is unconsciously done by covert hypnotists. If it makes you wonder what it is we are seeing then in the middle of the Hegelian synthesis, it is a scripted version, a legislated arithmetic to outlaw the middle / legislate the middle. Hegelian dialectic is thus a legend to pose extremes and force a choice between."

Researchers thus explain something that is nothing. Once an alternate reality is proposed, counterfeit parallels play it out. However the level of anestheticide to keep people sleeping must always increase. Make-up news, pseudo news projected from dome to brain in the sunny skies is sleeping, like having tea before a tsunami. Wheels within wheels form the psychosis present in citizens as a result of living in the 'shelter state' (Summary of Part II, A Case of Conscience). Ask whether the alternative too doesn't have an alternate. Multiverses pile up in the macro alters.

"Here's the bonee of torture. Take it that the *Bluebird* and *Artichoke* operations [PDF] are the outgrowth of

WWII intelligence operations against the Russians, informed by the Nazis. Agencies still feel required to match the latest contrivances of control among all parties. They induced amnesia in comatose states with primitive Seconal-Dexedrine-marijuana combinations. All they wanted was a truth drug! The same story at Gitmo with scopolamine. Sidney Gottlieb's Boston Mass Psychopathic Hospital led to MKDelta where everybody was getting high on the Gov. Addiction Research in Lexington levitated subjects with 77 straight days of LSD. They did to personality what Graf Welhausen did to Moses, which worked so good they started slipping it to strangers. Defenestrating germs and toxins at LSD expos went out the windows. The same boys followed Wasson to mushrooms who followed Hofmann to LSD. That's how Bob Hyde got Ted K. These geniuses connected all this to the brainwashed Korean POWs, and added torture, confinement.The induced confession and subsequent reeducations by the Chinese state were a no brain forerunner to the Red list, blue list, white list abductees to come. The hero of the [CIA] Allan Memorial Institute was director, D. Ewen Cameron, head of the American Psychiatric Association. You can see the new world order approaching with depatterning, amnesifying with combined sleep-electroshock, negative "psychic driving" [a feedback looped tape played in the ears over and over while drugged]. Sensory deprivation at the Society for the Investigation of Human Ecology led inexorably to John Lilly floating around stoned in his tank thinking he was a dolphin. Lots of them did the

dolphin tank, as occult a thing then as DMT is now to outsiders. Harold Wolff, President of the American Neurological Association and Lawrence Hinkle of the Gittinger Assessment System all ended up with Chomsky on the payroll with NLP in the pocket of new control."

We learned later the deep background to this, which I suppose none of us are hearing this for the first time. What's the probability of a people thousands of years before predicting for a people thousands of years after why America would care about Hebrew, Egyptian, Babylonian disorders? Psych-mytho-tics invents a new word for recombinant fanatics; the Suspicions themselves are suspicious and worse. Suspicions mounted in the conditions of psycho-chemical war among increased incidents of provocation. Everybody smoked, drank, injected, ingested amnestic fugue with those god- suspicious Americans.

"Those dissociations not being personal or individual, but corporate, whatever else the world system was, it coded a million layered alters with the highest wisdom awarded to anyone who would *know the world.* That's what the secret schools were about. All nations and groups were to be *responsible to the world,* meaning the coded, subjugated, prioritized alters layered in individual personalities. These were a metaphor of the social whole. The macro alters in society's head include *every* public figure. Abraham of ancient Ur knew the world system was dissociative, that's why he left. Ever

since then the urge to leave Ur and oppose its diverse voices and gods has been met with new efforts of control. In the coinage of sins against the world, they were to be held accountable to the *world*."

Hammond would not identify the perpetrators, but plenty of others did. In the Sexus, Nexus and Plexus of coercion, reality being a fan based unanimity, if *anything* they said is true all popular reality was destroyed. That's how Cheney got his name, de Sade, and Huysmans his imagination. Did it happen, is it true? You believe in political parties and leaders? You imagine someone unimaginably tortured every day of their life. Does that beg to be considered in the context of Gitmo prisoners given the zombie insanity drug and coerced with feeding tubes to keep them alive, then killed, then revived, over and over? Would you allow one person to be tortured forever if it would improve the lot of all people? One thing to be admired is the near perfection of the masks public figures wear, yet none are taken out of character. Cheney brutal, Reagan doting, Obama murderous. Were we to look for confirmation of reports and records in appendicies it is at least impressive to imagine someone faking them. So either way something is validated where the feel and style of reporting suggests the truth.

"Ultimately when you hear that some assassin heard "voices" it comes to be understood as code for something else as incomprehensible, as if we were to lay hands on

the head of some scientist who cut the antennae off Monarch butterflies and send *him* out into the desert headless, as a species of human medicine. "It was remarkable, the difference," Reppert said. "The ones without antennae still flew straight, but as a population they were flying in all different directions, compared to the population of migrants with intact antennae that was all going in a southwesterly direction."

"How this is done to people! Reppert and his team had been studying the ability of butterfly antenna to sense odors when they uncovered something surprising: When they clipped off the insects' antennae and tethered them in a flight simulator, the butterflies no longer flew in a uniform direction. Without their feelers, the butterflies lost the ability to navigate using the sun, as if they could no longer adjust their direction based on the time of day. The ability to navigate that enables the Monarch's life is analogous in humans to the boundaries of their learned identity stored collectively in personality, memory, culture. These boundaries include every aspect of the antennae produced from gestation, birth, infancy, through the stages of life. To interrupt these at any point to experiment for purposes of knowledge or control is to cut off the antennae of human identity. Then they will fly in all different directions."

The basis of Monarch programming was that different personality parts called alters could be created who do not know each other, but can take the body at different

times. The amnesia walls that built from trauma protect the abusers from being found out, and prevent front personalities who operate the body from knowing how the System of alters is being used. This shield of secrecy allows the operators to live and work around other people undetected. The front alters can be wonderful citizens, and the deep can be the monster, perfect scapegoats for high-profile rituals using intense trauma to force dissociation – a natural response in people faced with unbearable pain.

"Trauma-based mind control programming, systematic torture blocked the victim's capacity for conscious processing (through pain, terror, drugs, illusion, sensory deprivation, sensory over-stimulation, oxygen deprivation, cold, heat, spinning, brain stimulation, and often, near-death), then employed suggestion and classical operant conditioning with the most recent well-established behavioral modification principles. Thoughts implanted into the unconscious mind with directives and perceptions in newly-formed trauma-induced dissociated identities forced the victim to do, feel, think, or perceive things for the purposes of the programmer with no conscious awareness.
The Monarch butterfly learns where it was born (its roots) and it passes this knowledge via genetics on to its offspring (from generation to generation). This was one of the key animals that tipped scientists off, that knowledge can be passed genetically. Butterfly researcher Karen Oberhauser: "This is what science has

done: cutting the antennae off Monarch butterflies to prove "butterflies lost the ability to navigate using the sun." Antennae-less butterflies, antennae painted with black enamel, to block the sun, drift north, instead of south, ruining their molecular clock. "Insects can taste with their feet and smell with their antennae... it's sometimes difficult for us to even ask the right questions."

"Each isolated part of the psyche cocooned with walls of amnesia from memories impossible to consciously live with preoccupied techniques of conditioning. Whether externalization of hierarchy, DARPA narrative networks, or remote control technology, a hundred names, it was a war, a law to itself. That's why when Ginsburg asked Burroughs, "Bill, what's all this stuff about boys being hung in limestone caves?" the voices he heard and harmonically tuned through mind control mirror-reversals and interdimensional, Air-Water mind-control themes captivated audiences."

You don't write about this stuff without asides, which conspiracy or non seem a lot easier to read than these fantastic stories. The reasons for this are clear. The temperature of the water in the pot begins to steam. The frogs within, who have been there, do not know. To them the weather is balmy, unseasonable maybe, but pleasant. It is the same in every bubble. Can you believe our incredible good luck! The ones who perceive the danger

must have been thrown out by some accident. [Burroughs' experiences on *yage* and DMT were in fact the main influences on his work from *Naked Lunch* on, and the themes (aliens, creatures, language as a virus, typewriters transforming into cockroaches etc), and indeed his radical attempt at transforming the English language, all stem from his earlier tryptamine use" (William S. Burroughs: The Godfather of DMT"). But that is to take the high road of WB, who always slept with a gun at his head, and of course killed his wife with one, shot her in the head, although excused for it, after all he was *connected* in many shadowed events. Among the many Baals worshiped by the poet politic, (see Yeats and Baal), Burroughs familiar was Baal Peor, evident from the insane preoccupations of Naked Lunch after the first 30 or so pages. Back among the drugs, strange bedfellows of the ethnogenic, Jonathon Ott, *Entheogenic Drugs,* (*entheogen* meaning *god-generated-within)* had his home in NM burned by arson in March 2010 just as Tom Horn, foremost opponent of transhumanism had his burned in Montana in January 2011. Deception is no Simple].

-Through Dr. Franke we learned the particulars of antennae removal as the criminal acts of science were cataloged. He told so many and we were so busy writing them down only a fraction survived of the continual monocloidal taps. They admit to 120 heads of famous scientists on tap in the museums, but the real operations, whole factories where heads are hooked up

to the disinformation machines fed directly into the computer, both thoughts and speech, for many of them speak too, but they all think, gives a complete record of these thoughts. These are so vast they could only be compared to all the emails sent since the time began, a sufficient evil thereof. We took feverishly the materials of Lockerbie and Franke we have space for here, but of the general notes as they heads rapped, we only got partials, or half words, and since they were in many languages, sometimes the spellings are off, although we have tried to keep it to English mostly, so be a little forgiving at the abruptness.

> George Bush snakes, super soldier programming, mother wolves, gold and diamond bones, ascended machine technology, engraved bullets, enhanced rogues, psychopathic auto tuning, repetitious sound clips, .Asch conformity experiments , Münchausen syndrome by proxy, Pseudologia fantastica, meta stream capture, titanomachy, Jin and Faery chain, Captain Beefheart's Mother Ship heart, Pleiadian cultural infrapsychic incursion, dark side *Spielsberg* deconstructs, ZARG, Ubik, Kaznacheyev, Chimeras, Polyphemus, Coltrane , psychotron, Gaslighting the alien track base on Penang, Yé'iitsoh, Looking Glass facility, Tsiolkovsky, *Huai Nan Tzu*, US Naval Q552 cybernization, , noctilucent clouds, Welsbach material, Byzantine hybridomas, Porcelain Face Programming, microtubles as paramecium, reinforcement alters, biosystem waves, *Hazqiyal,* Kevin

Seasolts, *denial affirmation,* NESARA -Cryptozoology, Anarcho-Transhumanism, disinformation.com, Milking the Golem for H+, Nephilim pop, Smithsonian Coverup, Tigress kidnappings, identified child psychics, amount of oxygen processed in the blood determines psychic ability before project Manniquen, minced unconscious *lasav sav lasav kav lakav kav lakav, Sothli if a strongere comynge above overcome him, he schal tak a wey alle his armeris, in which he tristide, and schal dele abrood his spuylis.* **εὐαγγέλιον,** *La tua città, che di colui è pianta che pria volse le spalle al suo fattore,* Hegelian diabetes.

Live as one.
On tata menyon.
E. Pluribus unum bro.
Eine Welt!
Ein Volk

Jim Keith. In Your Head - Experiments into Remote Mind Control Techniques.pdf
L. Ron. Hubbard - The Brainwashing Manuel.Synthesis of the Russian Textbook on PsychoPolitics pdf 1955
Gillin, et. al. Mind Control Using Holography and Disassociation.pdf 2000
Walter Bowart. Operation Mind pdf 1978

Somehow the heads could switch identities in the middle of rapping and something completely different would come out. During the *Dzogchen- entrainment-secession and organization-entropy of* ***emergent factors*** sessions *of mindstream intentionality*, this came out of a medieval rabbi:

The supposition that תּועפות הרים denotes the pit-works (μέταλλα) of the mountains is an improbable, antithesis to מחקרי־ארץ, the shafts of the earth.

The derivation from יעף(ועף), κάμνειν, κοπιᾶν, also does not suit תועפות in Numbers 23:22; Numbers 24:8, for "fatigues" and "indefatigableness" are notions that lie very wide apart. כסף תּועפות of Job 22:25, "silver of fatigues," i.e., silver that the fatiguing labor of mining brings to light, means ascending summits of the mountains, after which כסף תועפות, Job 22:25, might also signify "silver of the mountain-heights." But the lxx render δόξα in Numbers and τὰ ὕψη τῶν ὀρέων in Job goes back to the root יף, וף, to stand forth, tower above, according to which it equals תופעות i.e., towerings, summits, prominences the highest perfection, a synonym of the Arabic mîfan, mîfâtun, a means of rising above, by climbing, which Hitzig renders: the teeth of mountains. Because Jahve is (cf. 1 Samuel 2:8), the Creator of all things, the call to worship is repeated in invitation, השׁתּחוה to stretch one's self out full length upon the ground, the proper attitude of adoration.

French Camp

Perhaps some will say, how dost thou know a road which thou hast not traveled full length--to which I say that we can see a road pretty correctly a considerable distance before us, and if we could not see before us at all, we should be stumbling almost at every step. (v).

A lot of lucky beasts fall from the sky, Buddha brambles we'd say. Where are they going? Anubis on guard. Pandemics no excuse! Wind sock high conscious god men side Sir Thomas on London Bridge. French camp went by truck to Dubuque wrapped end to end with iron lifts, then the whole back falls. Marks at least of sliding doors and windows would have been. Made it look grumpy. Our team reassembled with clamps and glue. Humphrey back on his rails looked like Le Corbusier. Everybody knows hermetically sealed only adds to the comfort. Not to worry. That's the parlance *where some angel catapults right in front of the eyes.* A whole train out of Europe, the globe. The French camp will be fun.

Can you believe it was to have taken only the French? When did co-signers keep their word? Amicus White Father (AWF) promised glands. Why did Ansel Adams ignore migrants? Why did Borges ignore Disappeareds? Stats suggest missing persons increased sixfold to 900,000 a year, 850,000 *juvenilios*. Illegals moved to Minnosota Mining to the Middle Complex (*Kidnapping For Scientific Betterment*). The silver lining revived the Boxcar Fund, saved Big Steel, seats for millions hauled, 100,000 boxcars in all, good for shares of *les Petits-Gris* , meaning Archuleta, or *Eisenaliens, or *iron ore* if such neolog appears. Highly allergenic to ammonia, years later these would die from it, the worst part of mythical horrors concocted below.

Regeneration, at least in its commencement, is a work of the mind, and when it first takes place, it has the lusts of the flesh, yea, all the evil inclinations to war against; and even ignorance itself, together with the temptations and allurements from without.

Whoever passes the coliseums with their corporate *wings thundering,* chariot *breastplates breathing iron,* should not think only martyrs lift the veil. Sir Stephen said, "when you worship Saturn you a post Weimar Moloch to hold its gods." Trade and Spend, Schneider, Mandarin, European, Pleidian. Cheap refrigerators, cheap gas? Maquiadores against the bones. Talk about government waste, the body underwent quadruple expansion. Fusion centers, post offices, generic buildings in the physical disappeared. into Adam Smith: "if he was to lose his little finger to-morrow, would not sleep at all that night, but provided he never saw them, could snore with the most utmost security over a hundred million of his brethren ruined, which destruction of that immense would seem less interesting than this paltry misfortune of his own." (*Theory of Moral Sentiments*). That was before Rocky Smith got high on time with the Mandarin clans. ET high. UCRC (Underground Cities and Residential Centers) were silent on this, a caveat where midnight airports *prove* the toy of Saturn is not a rocket, but cargo animated within whenever these colonial mysteries along the Archuleta Fault assembled. Above the 129 Bases in the Ten Sectors, Sir Stephen on Weimar comprehended the involvement of Orion and Sirius downtown. Falun Gong tracers of these implantation techniques were actively searching for people who could foresee the future, DNA specific. The big record of "Tussaud! the Musical" said,

"Are you ready?
Are your life forms prepared to receive those definitions that will terminate their larval existence?"

To be or not to be the gods was cool. Contradictory states opened for sleeping millions and billions of human seed and their llumined stem cells.

If the object in writing this was to gain the applause of men; thus to presume, so disappointed, such fiction written as some will not readily receive, however, on the other hand, having for a considerable time had pretty much the same ideas of the matter as you will find written down in this work, if you want to know, a train yard of boxcars full of Chinese guillotines being stored at US Military Bases - keep the engine running - I won't be a minute.

You want go oracoplankton? Maybe get a glimpse of Houston? Without the shell the webwork is not good to visit. That is to say, once the shells crack and the future is loosed, cracked shell divination Orc-acle has no place to return, and lest it be cast into the void floats indeterminately about waiting to find a body, which we infer from those explosions in the desert. Divination beyond unsaid, allows us to see these *nosce te ipsum* pyromancy of ancient kings long used to inquire by fire.

Lots of folks still say Encephaliticality. Brain swelling made visible in science and folklore dub "Bluehenge," after the 27 Welsh stones that lead to them, When the stones disappeared the holes remained, like the shells, but all there is now the ditch.

The Delphi omachines practice this oppossibility back down the ages wild, the waves, the belly of a bear sung by the famous telling the means to know *gnōthi seauton.*

Temet nosce is a blank screen on the dome of the world. Oracles sold this telepathy with external attachments to produce it. They applied hot iron to their backs to read the cracks. *Gnōthi seauton*! *gnōthi seauton*! In the mirror they cried, thrice, to see what's underneath. It gave them a picture of their lives.

Scute Transformation and third brain queries of ventral surface in the fornix made a habit of hybrid speech. Electrolyte excretion catalyzed the prognathous jaw. Interventricular foramina that transmit cranial nerves, connecting lateral ventricles and the third, functioned as a posterior heart.

Subdermal Leathery Scutes

Orcs and lizards are relate this exaggeration. Thought lizards lost their legs that Orcs retained. Kinetic skulls united pairs of copulatory organs in scaly skin. Black surmounted insectoid dermal crystalate ossifications of rib and pectoral girdle fused. Eventual fusion expanded contracted ribs.

Epidermal scutes of leather skin do NOT have the same composition or pattern as dermal bone, which explains the craquelure and quaking of the whole. The "shell" of dorsal carapace, is a thin ventral plastron that *alligators* as a synonym for craquelure; finer networks of cracks aging shrink the shell to a brittle record of the conditions which cover any fine lobster.

The posterior skull is emarginated to allow a muscle. High domes result. Any measurements for height and snout-vent result from dermal ossifications in most generic tetrapods. The hinged plastron of shell closure paired with the copulatory organs resulted in mongrelization, one based upon the Repertory Grid technique and the other on Bezier curves.

Following the latest viral challenge of fat redistribution and lipid peroxidation in rats treated with an angiotensin-converting enzyme (ACE) inhibitor (lisinopril), lasted up to 10 months. Uninephrectomized rats develop hypercholesterolemia typical of chronic renal failure compared with sham-operated rats lisinopril-treated uninephrectomized. The weight of the peri-renal rat was significantly less in the untreated compared to the uninephrectomized meaning those with a sham operation. There was a shift of heat-protecting unilocular adipocytes in multilocular fat cells untreated. Hydrocephalic Virus brain outbursts occur in the thrice vaccinated who are the physical catch of the microburst. We provide more of this:

Further Notes Toward Earth Orcprothangon of the Evolutionary Dentation Trends and Scutes of the Oraclar Subclades

Précis

The positional skull appears large because it is emarginated to allow muscle attachment. High domes thus result. Measurements given for height and snout-vent length are for the larger individuals. Theories of cloned carapace from dermal ossifications are a result of mongrelization.

Some think the paired copulatory organs, prevalent in both bird and mammal origin derived from the bird, for the beaks precede the formation of teeth, in the young, but parental care is indifferent in these creatures who go to ground to breed, a chief reason after living in mountains to which they have returned after centuries. Resembling an upright ant, the Orc works hard to justify its existence, though it is now predominantly defensive in most generic tetrapods. Two types of representation are compared: one based upon the Repertory Grid technique and the other based upon Bezier curves.

Three lineages of reptile independent of fully evolved marine life (meosaurs, pleiosaurs, and ichthyosaurs) spawned Orcs (mammals plus bird) independently over 100 million years apart. Bird ancestors from these arose from precursors of the dinosaurs in the Jurassic. Only reptiles that survived into the Cenozoic belong to presently living orders.

Thecodonts are the ancestors of both dinosaurs and crocodylimorphs (crocodiles, alligators etc). Based on some morphological differences between birds and theropod dinosaurs, and on a temporal gap in the fossil record of several million years from the last theropod to the first bird, proposals that birds did not evolve from theropods but rather from thecodonts actually only introduce an even larger temporal gap since the youngest thecodont fossil is much older than the youngest theropod. The theropod-bird theory is by far the best supported one in paleontology.
http://richarddawkins.net/forum/viewtopic.php?start=60&t=9766

Following an uninephrectomy the remnant kidney undergoes a compensatory growth apparently regulated by a humoral renotropic factor(s). Our studies were carried out to assess the role of renal and hepatic tissue in the generation of such a renotropic factor(s) in surgical excision of one kidney

Here we examine the effect of chronic renal dysfunction induced by uninephrectomy on fat redistribution and lipid peroxidation in rats treated with an angiotensin-converting enzyme (ACE) inhibitor (lisinopril) for up to 10 months. Uninephrectomized rats developed fat redistribution and hypercholesterolemia typical of chronic renal failure when compared with sham-operated rats or lisinopril-treated uninephrectomized rats. The weight of the peri-renal fat was significantly less in the untreated compared to the lisinopril-treated uninephrectomized rats or those rats with a sham operation. We also found that there was a shift of heat-protecting unilocular adipocytes to heat-producing multilocular fat cells in the untreated uninephrectomized rats.

The paper applies the context of research to define simple dichotomous terms. The validity of the proposed set of eight descriptors is established by reference to the various classification tasks.

These include the unassisted assignment of Orc to specific categories by experienced subjects, the same task undertaken by inexperienced subjects assisted by rules, the classification of representations of craquelure by a neural network, and by discriminant analysis.

Back to the beginning of this prodiginon these Hydrocephalic Virus brain vectors
are the physical catch of the microburst and the gas.

2. Going down the list sounds like contradiction until we realize that **Encephalitic Reality** is invisible, but its footprints are not hard to see. Researchers have dubbed such sites as "Bluehenge," after the color of the 27 Welsh stones that were laid up to make a path, but all that remains of the site is the ditch. The stones disappeared but the path of holes remains.

Awareness shrinks itself into body functions. That this threatens environmental disaster is obvious, as its ordure attracts us like comedians who needed a laugh every twenty seconds, but who otherwise turn to foible, turn Lenin and Marx into a postage stamp, the Abkhazian Lennon and Groucho Marx to fulfill our stereotypes of themselves which we caw at for its turpitude. Some psychology! This ugliness transformed to the good destroys the good, but dentary enlargement and postdentary reduction do not explain all its subclades.

In posterior we go back down the ages in earth among peoples like the wild, because it comes between and enables our life of oppossibility, the belly of a bear, the belly of a bear, the waves, the sing song sing of the **Oracle famous for telling himself the means to know him. The p**roverb applied to this boast, Latin of the Apollo temples and the Delphi omachines, *gnōthi seauton.* You want to hear about an oracle, this attractive *nosce te ipsum· temet nosce* named for their omachines. Oracles were a blank screen on the architecture of the world. But we explore the primitive Urk or as we like to call him Ork.

To say Oracles sold themselves the value of telepathy and took external attachments to produce it. The orcs prefer that version of pyromancy where ancient kings or anybody could inquire of the oracle questions about the result of some thing they proposed. This proposal was answered variously by applying a hot iron to a tortoise shell and reading the interpretation of the resulting cracks from a handbook until Orcs cracked themselves, that is their shells, or in the case of the profane, their spirits, donned for the interim of their lives, they loosed and lay beside the fire. Shell here is the way we picture spirit, which usually can't be seen. Once these shells were loosed they were cracked, but that does not deny that the orc without its shell, naked, is a spectacle of white mottled webwork we have elsewhere divined. So cracked the shell answered the proposal with only one proviso, that after divination the Orc had no shell to return to, it having been demolished, what is what we refer to in all those explosions in the desert taken as heat lightening. Divination stepped beyond the natural and we can only plummet it by reference to the unseen in the unsaid of the said, which the prophet L has allowed us to follow with his rehearsals.

The Scute Transformational kidney and third brain queries on the ventral surface of the fornix near the interventricular foramina interconnecting the lateral ventricles and the third ventricle produce in these cases a complex of hybrid speech. Connected in the electrolyte excretion of the prognathous jaw, the displacement in function of a posterior heart.

Subdermal Leathery Scutes

More specifically, Orcs, lizards and snakes are related by exaggeration. Snakes were once thought lizards that lost their legs that Orcs retained and stood up. All were united by kinetic skulls, paired copulatory organs and dry, scaly skin, not to speak of the forked tongue that "smells" odors in the environment.

The Orc classically displayed a helmet and the mantle of a dark carapace, mostly black, surmounted with an insectoid crysalate, a sheen of dermal ossifications of ribs and parts of the pectoral girdle fused. Eventual fusion of these plates with the skeleton produced a marked difficulty in expanding and contracting the ribs. How this contributes to the Orc development is soon obvious.

The "shell" of this dorsal carapace has a thin ventral plastron. These epidermal scutes are made of leathery skin, but the scutes and dermal bones do NOT have the same composition or pattern, which explains the craquelure and ultimate quaking of the whole structure. The term alligatoring is used by some people as a synonym for craquelure; others distinguish the two, using craquelure for finer networks of cracks associated with aging when the shell shrinks and becomes more brittle. Craquelure furnishes a record of the environmental conditions the shell has experienced in its lifetime, The carapace of the exoskeleton covers the body just as it would any well developed lobster. The greatest help and hindrance to the Orc is this outer shell, of which the craquelure is its most appealing feature

The hinged plastron once allowed either closure of the shell or its removal. That the posterior skull appears large is because it is emarginated to allow muscle attachment. High domes result from this. Any measurements given for height and snout-vent length are for the largest individuals likely to be encountered. Theories of a cloned carapace result from dermal ossifications in most generic tetrapods. Some think the paired copulatory organs, prevalent in both bird and mammal origin, a result of mongrelization.

Derived from its bird origin, beaks precede the formation of teeth in the young, but parental care is indifferent in these creatures who go to ground to breed, a chief reason Orcs live in mountains to which they have returned after centuries. Resembling an upright ant, the Orc works hard to justify its existence, though it is now predominantly defensive. I know some orcs and am interested in their language habits. There is a lot written of orc talk but what i say comes from life.

Orcs afflict themselves with an engobe. Much conversation is diatribe but separate the speech from what they write, because an

orc is really a timid speaker unless really stirred, but as a writer the orc is a fearless and fearsome adversary, able to twist literally everything said to it's own advantage, so there is some intelligence in it, but perverted. Any orc writing will exhibit the logical, rhetorical fallacies galore. But on to the details.
Examples of this are its continual concern with the petty details of its body, what it eats, when it bathes, what it watches on TV, what it thinks about its digestion, its bowel movements, its sex habits, its imagination. The orc will tell you everything you don't want to know much as if you were its mother and cared very much if the ostial fluid was dark or the tooth decayed

Another example is the way it covers its type pad with acronyms, OMG, WTF. Really a complete catalogue of these would be interesting. Any ideas?

The petty affects of its language are aggressive. It will threaten to "rip out your..." name calling is very prevalent too. The heaping up of abuse, like a kind of food fight with feces. Reminds of Swift a little. Does anyone think there an orc component to minimalist poetry or art? You know where the words are cut midsentence and the nouns mutated into fractive elements like in vernacular speech but exaggerated so?
Of course all this leads to whether or what the orc meditates on, that is it's inner thought processes. Don't want to make this too long, but there's lots more. Can I get a witness? Heaere here then is ti pure science, no characters, blue men or green, not e'en subterre warriers of comics. That's what we get from the brine where the waters come salty from heaven.

AS FAR AS THE ORCS GO THIS removal of the shell was achieved by DESSICATION, the same also INDUCED in the

dissemination of radar gaps, antennas. There must be a special place for taking metaphor seriously in the transverse cerebral thrombosis.

Cracking or fine cracking "Craquelure" implies a finer crack than the French "fissure"="crack/fissure", and also tends to imply a network of intersecting cracks (cracks due to ground movement and settlement might be preferentially oriented, but shrinkage cracks would be in all directions). In other contexts one might talk of "hairline cracks as a fissure is (supposedly and initially) considerably larger than the cracking that subsequently occurs in the flow itself or as a sun crack, shrinkage crack, mud crack you see in drought areas.

The orc's limbs require further investigation (fig. 7). The initial application of silver leaf still exists in many areas, covered with a layer containing ochre, lead white and black iron oxide pigments that seems to have served as an initial green glaze over the silver leaf. A second, light green glaze applied thereafter may be contemporary or of later date; this second glaze contains shellac, terre verte and Prussian blue, with traces of calcium sulfate and calcium carbonate.

The presence of copper in this layer, a trace of copper carbonate pigment. This layer was seen after solvent cleaning and lifting of later, darker layers with a scalpel. The sculptured relief of scales on the Orc's skin was shaded with a darker glaze that has not been analyzed but most likely employs more Prussian blue. A varnish that is probably mastic was next applied; its craque- lure followed that of the layers found under it, indicating that it was contemporary with them. The **craquelure** of succeeding, darker layers is different, indicating a later date for them. These darker layers contain spirit varnish, perhaps mastic; determination of whether there are pigments in them is incomplete, and it is not certain whether they are additional colored glazes or simply coats of varnish.

Note:

The lengths given for total length (TL) and snout-vent length (SVL) are for the largest individuals likely to be encountered. The odd feature of this shell surface on such a malign creature is that it is honeycombed, rosemaled, decorated with paintings that resemble nothing as much decorated immigrant chests.

Fondness for colorful ornamentation in the bone is evident in fine examples of painted furniture, Their practicality demonstrated by the simple lines and sturdy construction of such pieces made for everyday arched panels enclosing parrot-like birds with tulips and fuchsias, The ground color is a reddish brown. Amish blue and cypress green. Designs common to the other counties are: arched panels unicorns rampant among tulips and pomegranates; square panels flower sprays rising from a vase, circular medallions overlaid with six-pointed stars, tulips and carnations,

There is conflict between the archeology and anthropology. Understand by anthropology we should read Orcopology. When it was found that these creatures survived even the settling of places like Kansas, where they once ranged, moved up the mountains, although not just in the US, it began to be apparent that they were more intelligent than first thought, as if they had hired public relations managers to neutralize their previous identities. Archeology, anthropology, politics, and finally psychology became the inquiry, and for all this the shields are the best informant.

First, in dimension, the shield is a generally spherical chest plate covering chest and midsection, rising up and attaching over the shoulders and down the back. In that sense it is a carapace. Once it was detached or detachable, but over the course of its survival it is theorized that Orcs had to leave shields under duress, and in all weathers and circumstances so that they literally fused with the scute, the dermal bone underneath. The aesthetic appeal of these chest plates is a major artistic interest so that it has been compared with archaic Greek Vase painting, and even more so because it is the forces of nature that decorate. To what degree the Orc cooperating individually in the making of these designs is a more difficult study. The shield seems to identify the Orc to which it belongs, for they are by no means alike. The relation of shield to Orc is both personal and so intimate. The shield is also a mask to frighten enemies and inspire the imagination of friends, so that it is not too extreme to say that the Orc *is* its shield. As in aboriginal lands the shields together tell a communal story, decipherable if we had enough of it to tell. As it is we have as it were some words and paragraphs out of large storybook. Still these tell enough of the Orc wars, their gods, rather Norse like in effect. If all this seems strange to designs simply produced by nature, let it be compared with the fossil record that also tells a story, a grand epic, even as geology is, of the forces that shape land, if not sky. How these natural forces interacted on the shields, making them figurative and narrative, is the concern of this paper.

American English is a dying language in many circles replaced by Anglo-Orkish. This phenomenon was described by the well-known linguist and philologist J.R.R. Tolkein, and discussed in his works, "The Hobbit", and "The Lord of the Rings". He goes to some trouble to discuss orkish language and culture, particularly in

Bilbo's passage through the Misty Mountains; Pippin and Merry's captivity, and Frodo and Sam's journey into and through Mordor. There is a further reference in the scouring of the Shire, when the hobbits take note of the "lots of rules and orc-talk," due to an orkish influence brought in by Saruman and his agents.

In the appendix to Lord of the Rings, he mentions that "**orkish speech is even more coarse than I have rendered it",** but that he does not need to detail it any further, since examples are commonly encountered among the orc-minded.

Very possibly, he could be referring to references to people in replacement of most English adjectives by a vulgar term for the reproductive act, or a more specific variant referring to a female parent. I don't like to criticize other people's language: I've confined myself to refusing to speak orkish myself. How resistible is linguistic change? Cited from:
http://confutus2.blogspot.com/2005_09_01_archive.html

Orc Talks

A lot of people think Orcs like speaking, but this is not true A lot of people think they can arrive at the unknown through disorder. Black scale evolutionists prove have proved a reptilian likeness.

Herbs for Orcs: The Rise and Fall

Three lineages of reptile independent of fully evolved marine life (meosaurs, pleiosaurs, and ichthyosaurs) spawned Orcs (mammals plus bird) independently over 100 million years apart. Bird ancestors from these arose from precursors of the dinosaurs in the Jurassic. Only reptiles that survived into the Cenozoic belong to presently living orders.

> Thecodonts are the ancestors of both dinosaurs and crocodylimorphs (crocodiles, alligators etc). Based on some morphological differences between birds and theropod dinosaurs, and on a temporal gap in the fossil record of several million years from the last theropod to the first bird, proposals that birds did not evolve from theropods but rather from thecodonts actually only introduce an even larger temporal gap since the youngest thecodont fossil is much older than the youngest theropod. The theropod-bird theory is by far the best supported one in paleontology. http://richarddawkins.net/forum/viewtopic.php?start=60&t=9766

The Orc is a predation or orc talk is when it knocks at your door. Dare open and it sticks out a moon, which if one attends, is the exact effect of Orc upon men. Orcs embarrasses all who see. We love the hated thing.

The orc will tell you everything you don't want to know, much as if you were its mom and cared whether the ostial fluid was dark, the tooth decayed. Orifices, organs, castrate ridicule of parents, units! preoccupation with dirt, mucus, digestion. Petty affects of its written tongue are subbestive. It will threaten to "rip out your..." (anatomy part). Name calling prevalent. The heaping of abuse, like a fight with it references orifices, women as dogs, men as their offspring the replacement of most adjectives for the vulgar Orc of the act. An Orc component of minimalist art fractures, cut midsentence, nouns mutate in vernacular. It covers its type pad with acronyms. Really a complete catalogue of these would not be interesting.

Some have compared this debasement to Amer English, where English is Orkish and student and prof alike orc go to the heart of the dying culture Tollmer enabled a metaphorical demise.

Is Orkish a living or a dying tongue? In many circles, it is replaced by Anglo-Ork, Franc-Ork, Germ-Orkish so it is coming global. There is a further reference in the scouring of the Shire, where hobbits take note of the "lots of rules and orc-talk", due to an orkish influence brought in by Saruman and his agents. In the appendix to Lord of the Orcs "orkish speech is even more coarse than I have rendered it", but that does not need to detail it any further, since examples are commonly encountered among the orc-minded. This coarseness is not merely in the articulation of sibilants, fricatives and stops but in the semantics, word choice as well. It is the jinn, they say, who whisper into the ears of suicide-bombers

We can read this literally as the act of generation and passing of learned behaviors of a being divided from itself and the natural world, which science now confirms. short tempered, sullen, and prone to action rather than thought

the orc is demeaned by many of his closest fans, oddly denigrated as ungrammatical but one feels this true more of the fan than the Orc. the alleged bad spelling emotion, primitive usages of clone fighting, have a fan mag where they dispense advice to wannabes of gaming out.

Following an uninephrectomy the remnant kidney undergoes a compensatory growth apparently regulated by a humoral renotropic factor(s). Our studies were carried out to assess the role of renal and hepatic tissue in the generation of such a renotropic factor(s) and surgical excision of one kidney.

Here we examine the effect of chronic renal dysfunction induced by uninephrectomy on fat redistribution and lipid peroxidation in rats treated with an angiotensin-converting enzyme (ACE) inhibitor (lisinopril) for up to 10 months. Uninephrectomized rats developed fat redistribution and hypercholesterolemia typical of chronic renal failure when compared with sham-operated rats or lisinopril-treated uninephrectomized rats. The weight of the peri-renal fat was significantly less in the untreated compared to the lisinopril-treated uninephrectomized rats or those rats with a sham operation. We also found that there was a shift of heat-protecting unilocular adipocytes to heat-producing multilocular fat cells in the untreated uninephrectomized rats.

This did not appear in the *Journal of Unlikely Entomology* as planned.

The Virtual Madman Prophet Monster Video Game Play Killer Update Review / Madman Prophet Backpack / Rant History of Murder Prophets from Cho to Loughner: **An interview taken with the view of investigating the motives of societicide. Please enter your code name here or join for $7.95 a month. Speech Duet Given at the 2012 Cybernautic Convention, Cy-Naun**

This is a game where we practice to learn to kill, A game that happens to someone else meaning it's for real. Be part of the video, the prophet said, had we only known he would kill. The prophet untouched reaches out to us. What would Bin Laden do?

Out of the game we fear if you act you're wrong. In the game, wrong coming and going, victims moan. This culture, half in love with monsters, entertains a hundred million on TV killed, eclipsed however by billions in the video world.

Say agents are to blame, that pterodactyl made a nest and laid a steel egg in the breast. Say the best lacked all conviction, that the worst were filled, temperature rising in these crimes, even if the failures to communicate are as the psychologist says, paranoid, and need medication.

I. Video Game Practice

If all this seems opaque so is the indictment of the real we know and maybe love in a society taken to boil. Crying madman's not enough, cry psychotic or neurotic, bipolar manic, but not despotic, unless you mean psychiatric. "Once bipolar, always" means run, but you can't hide, unless you make the psychiatrist cry, then you are dismissed.

Whether man's humanity to man is a cure, the generic being dead, or killed by the man who also killed the earth we will learn. Among connections not to make, this raving, *you have never felt a single ounce of pain your whole life. Do you know what it feels like to be humiliated and be impaled upon a cross and left to bleed to death for your amusement?*

Each with dark reason, institutes with theirs indict the atmospheres. That language describes the southern hemisphere, shocking language that the crucifieds are everywhere. The madman is a treatise on ecology and theology with the suffering of the poor. Who is he speaking for, that dark mind? *Do you know what it feels like to be torched alive?* We set opposing statements side by side. Never take the ravings of a madman seriously. Take them as seriously as your own body.

We individuals are good to live and die apart. Innocent, we will not fight, nor go ungentle to ungood night. People have their defenses down who live in Anywhere Land. Moralists ask what society we would have if you have to lock a monster down. Had we known ahead the siege, that Bin Laden would destroy, we'd have acted say instead of videoing Cho.

Admiring the monster the video admits Rimbaud. Poets accuse us all, blind rage against the particular and the whole. Victims and the decadents they stand in place of, read first world rich, are, in their effect upon the monster, its creation. For who does not sympathize with nihilism in the liberation? That done, none, no none thinks because they're not on the news they are suffering.

This game has something for all.

After the fact of violence, authorities feel gang safe to announce they knew the monster, how good or bad it was. Maybe he died or killed or not. Gangs cry out against Moslem assailants. Moralists, Rushdie, no prophet, knows this idea false, or more kindly, fict. Nobody imitates him because of the danger, but they imitate Pinter by the score, rage against the west. Who wants to die for madmen prophets?

II.

A history from Longmeyer back to Cho

Virtual ignorance is a defense authorities have against games. There are a "hundred billion chances" not to know. Plausibly denied they wouldn't know. How could they know? Did you know? Fragments burst into minds. There was nothing they could do. Rationalizations, even if legally old, act on false positives in the memories of those who perp. The blind eye turns stereotype to life, just a fantasy madman in a Mercedes.

Bush in Iraq .
Bush in Iraq .
to void onslaught.
Sit on your hands.
Go out. Look back.

To win the game and be like the crucified of every nation, you should be an adult to play. Stakes are hundreds of millions high to know *what it feels like to dig your own grave.* That's why videos are made, otherwise the whole way of *crucifying others in order to live* is in doubt. It's in doubt, the whole way of turning the blind eye that many suffer so a few may enjoy (591). In the backpack of the virtual Mon, Ellecuria and the Bonhoefferin: *It is easy to regard the oppressed and needy as those who are to be saved and liberated, but it is not easy to see them as saviors and liberator.*

Do not think that freedoms are abuse, that freedom to debase has a social use? We have freedoms to call names that pretend lawlessness Do you know what inverts the law? Lions and snakes. They correct your freedom to wander drunk. There is a freedom to be profane till someone pulls a gun.

Freedom's taken,
Freedom's will
Up against Necessity's No.

Popular histories for the gullible, those mad panaceas, those cathartic OD's, are a joke on the game. If everything goes as planned in the *idealistic frenzied individualism and idealism so characteristic of Western civilization, or at least of its elites, all the selfishness borne by this notion is but the reverse of its exaggeration* (Ellecuria).

The video prophet anthology takes disorder well. It is not prone to madness like Collins, Thompson, Swift or Smart, the suicidal depression of Crane, Lowell, Hemingway and Plath. Drugs, madness, suicide can stop it, but aren't enough for murder.

Rimbaud is in the **backpack** too: *The poet makes himself a visionary through a long prodigious and rational disordering of all the senses. Every form of love, of suffering, of madness; he searches himself, he consumes all the poisons in him keeping only their quintessences.* Yahoo, the impulse strikes the poor man rich. Inducing disorder rationally hides the frenzied individualist: *"the soul has to be made monstrous...to make oneself a visionary."*

Surfeit of monsters,
I can't make up my mind,
reptilian likenesses...

the self like an animal...*there are no hard distinctions between what is real.* (Pinter's *Nobel*)

You can play the game at home in the online savage communities and sites, or "troll" at divergent dyings of the light, flood'em up email so to speak to just shut'em up. Anti-authority is not so bad. Father is worse than Sylvia's "Dad." Blog ethics threaten body parts, give death, dismember. Apprentices play the video part to parcel anger. "Injustice," is indifferent from the rant in verse of Pinter's blurred distinction. Many have pirated copies of the game.

Game scholars think attitudes of scatology provoke revenge. Anger, pedophilia, loneliness, murder those icons we are not supposed to name. They are not themselves icons, but the icons follow along. Debased speech celebrants practice praise for testing the limits. How many times can networks link game shows, chains and guns in one big bite? In his Nobel stickup Pinter says his art has *no hard distinctions between what is real and what is unreal, between what is true and false. It can be both true and false.* Pinter wants *a citizen to ask: What is true? What is false?* The exploration of reality through art, loose talk is the same for all the lost.

A Defense

We who deny the video prophet's mad excuse of our complicity in the event, as though primary, secondary, tertiary acts take seriously the message of revenge, that we ignore, are certain that the death of crucifieds has never penetrated this world. Video mad prophets take off in air where they help to recognize such things, but there is a fear it will spawn more copy cats.

When the video people turned the murder game on, and revenged all who would play into **one Virtual Mon**, a difference occurred from drama past. When you saw Hamlet on Macbeth, Oedipus, you left the theatre drained, aware and more humane. But when you leave the arcade strong, you feel invincible, think cars imaginary and yourself supernumerary.

Who needs the arcade, play at home! Play it all over again, but eventually it leads to this, pack a gun. That's what one friend did. A freshman hazing put two guns in his pack and headed out to school. You think it bad judgment. They will take you to jail for packing plastic, but if the gun is real pass by.

Beware neat packages murderers won't have to define. Think why nobody talked back, fought back, retook, attacked attack. Nuance the story administrators say, "we cannot let the horror define us," promise "to prevent anything like that again." Deflecting criticism from themselves officials pointed at sin, stopped showing the video so other murders wouldn't remake themselves, which suggests they will. Courts responsible for that, courts psychiatric, hospital officials all pointed. We broke no law of the video whose insight and judgment were normal, even if they were mad. It wasn't criminal, it wasn't health, you cannot compel dark thoughts. Wait till they get worse. Dimmed lights cannot feel the suicide, murder vibe. What should they do?

You idiot. People at the screen are ready for the next best thing. **One thought it a joke when the head next to him blew off. It's the fault of something greater, a cabbage giant so divine we cannot define it, a cannibal monster that looks in the eye, a beauty that impersonates desire.** Reality is not a fault to confess. People die for whom we could all be willing to be killed, pundits lament, but nobody is going to do anything against this loss except talk. Talk is entertainment. I saw a memorial of the slain; tears flowed down my face. This culture expressed a common anesthetic not to awake to the world, not wake enough to save. Along came a spider, a monster entertainer, and sat down to frighten. Gunfire popcorn.

III.

I have a friend who videos the short circuit brain. designed a class in school where he could play. Invited to the honor society before those days, his math went to D, his favorite AP history C and the state champion was declared ineligible. That's when he rode his bike to school and hit some cars, sudden stops, just avoidances, nicks of things, broke tires and fractured an arm he denied until the pain got strong. Among the classes this is video game. Its victims are famous for their post mortems which everyone justifies.

The video has a second act,
an awareness for victims to not be so much
the monster that those who ignore every symptom make
unclear distinction between the false and the fact.
In Game the monster cannot see its eye,
can't recognize action as act.

In the second act fathers hold sons to account, not the first. There fatherhood, disgraced, destructed, disrespected in the video prophet's play that mimics demolitions accomplished against fathers by their accusers in the list of cultural woes, are all the protection against these things that was ever had.

Cabbage Patch Head Game College Song

I say
we're not
supposed to play
the online game at home,
the savage troll that's not so bad,

the anti-authority of Sylvia's "Dad,"
who the dying of the light shuts up,
gives death and threatens parts.
Dismember
the apprentices!
with rants in verse
distinctive pirate copies play
the video prophet's mad excuse,
that serious message of revenge,
the death of the crucified
that penetrates earth.

Video prophets take off in air
to recognize such things,
but mad prophets spawn more copy cats
of all who play the Virtual Man
in Hamlet and Macbeth,
who left the theatre drained.
When videos turn humane,
you leave the arcade strong,
cars are imaginary, you are supernumerary
and that is the college song.

Unlikely Stories II, November 2011.

Subfornical Organ

These letters reflect the Subfornical Organ debate between Rubino del Sur and Peter FrigginFreund on the new organ practices that became part of our day.

Dear Mr. Sur:

I take the assertion that **PhysMyth** could pee with its mouth to be mere confusion of orifice, not a symbol of society and art so much as a cannibalism of its government, of which complex urinary speech affects neither.

To say that it split off a transformational kidney and evolved a third brain gives us grave reservations about reviewing your work which shows no sign of external standards or review.

Your,
P. Friggin-Freund, DDS

Dear Dr. Friggin-Freund:

It is the essence of *Bibliotosis* sir, where a societal hybrid turns its kidney into a brain, that secretude of peptide mind and posterior heart in uric speech that pees with its mouth. When the kidney had passed onto the Web, no further analogy evolved. It were harsh indeed to say they had magical properties akin to the urim and thummim when it walked with giants on the earth. This supposes memories were retained of its expulsion. Spirits with bodies, bodies with spirits, the upper classes still believe them. It was a shock to the establishment when first dug up and the shields displayed, which argued something had been missed.

As a counterfeit wolf with a wig would pass for a bear, not that a wolf assumes to call the bear fake, it represents a series of attitudes and prerogatives that dare to define a new reality utterly different from that ordinary one of caves and holes and black blood. It has gone global, and while it looks like a man, it is no more a man as classically defined than it ever was. Please allow us to forego at this time saying exactly what is a man. Change the appearance and you change the life. Not so, but it seems so.

I am,

Rubino del Sur

Dear Reubino:

Have you invented this literature?
Let me suggest you circulate your fantastic physiology among those magazines which can give a fuller sense of what external standards obtain, and please find a local physiology workshop of peer-criticism. Both exercises will impart some humility, which I, for one, find notable in its absence in writing that I find so far from that nature.

Sincerely,
P. Friggin-Freund DDS

Dear Dr. FrigginFreund:
Physiology is a malady of vasoconstrictive blood that created this language dysfunction of anti-diuretic stuff. The odor voids the bismuth substitute. Science has argued long and loud about PhysMyth, but even those workers who wore radiometric monitors were caused to suppurate.

The hairless homosaps proved not to be so unevolved as first thought. Surely you can see how linguists invented this **link to the uric world**. Posterior heart and third brain! Take it as you will. Fluids were needed to de-verb that inner world from sneeze.

Squirts! Innard verse! Opposites! Uresis had social effects. Volumes of spine poety! PhysMyth fled the glycemic. Anti-diuresis cooked crystal in the shell, spread to the brain! That explains the *double need* to hold it in. Praxis compressed a carapace to put the bit down, but won't it come up?

The body is white mottle, spindle shanked. Which is why it grew a shell to give it hide. The shell outside went under rib as leather scute overlay. This lasted until it peeled. Naked or not, nobody has seen it. Further decadence of this world perused in many places averts eyes from the flash and from revulsion. This is the fifth placement. I would stop writing this stuff if I could figure out what it is about.

Yours truly,
Marino Rubino del Sur

1. **Page 1: Title Page** (Title only: *The Annotated History of the World*)
2. **Page 2: Table of Contents**
3. **Page 3: I. Six Li'l Reactors** (Break after "...six nukes.")
4. **Page 4: The Nuke Family** (Break after "What's wrong with him?")
5. **Page 5: The Sea Change** (Break after "set back to back.")
6. **Page 6: The Gates of Sense** (Break after "Sleep.")
7. **Page 7: The Poisoned Ear** (Break after "porches of the EAR (th).")
8. **Page 8: The Alarm** (Break after the second "ADAM ADAM")
9. **Page 9: The Angels of Orc** (Break after "flames of Orc.")
10. **Page 10: The Death Trumpets** (Break after "harness up and dive")
11. **Page 11: The Radioactive Reef** (Break after "except for the eyes.")
12. **Page 12: Tritium!** (Break after "Tritium! Tritium! Tritium!")
13. **Page 13: The Elite Underground** (Break after "contaminated in their tombs.")
14. **Page 14: The Path to North Canada** (Break after "Everything long since d. and birds starved.")
15. **Page 15: Bio-Magnification** (Break after "mushroom concentrate.")
16. **Page 16: The Good News of 137** (Break after "Bq per body weight sought-")
17. **Page 17: The Curie and the Bq** (Break after "make them readable")
18. **Page 18: The Cesium Chair** (Break after "Radioactive isotopes of cesium are extremely active compared")
19. **Page 19: The Human Fire** (Break after "limbs were fire.")

20. **Page 20: The Geiger Counter** (Break after "reading you can hear?")
21. **Page 21: The Spectre's Voice** (Break after "a voice came forth.")
22. **Page 22: The Banana Click** (Break after "went the banana")
23. **Page 23: The Cesium Pop** (Break after "went the Cesium 137 pops")
24. **Page 24: Extreme Saturation** (Break after the "ZZZZZZZZZZ" wall)
25. **Page 25: The Numerology of 137** (Break after "Kubla Khan,")
26. **Page 26: The Dragon Arises** (Break after "at midnight arose,")

The Annotated History of the World

Table of Contents

I. Six Li'l Reactors

Six li'l reactors
Was sittin' in lead,
Three got sick
so the other ones went,

They sent for the doctor,
but the doctor said,
get them little meltdowns
some explosion bread.

Tepco's little baby
had a meltdown meltdown
Tepco's little baby
on a meltdown sped.

The Nuke Family

Once upon a time there were six nukes.

A momma nuke, a poppa nuke and a MOX nuke baby who lost their cores in earth.

Who's been stealing my core, said number four?

Who knows where they are?

Radiation flows from them like an issue of blood.

The north Pacific beyond is the woman of EARth

Tritium!

Tritium!

What's wrong with him?

The Sea Change

He’s undergone a complete sea change

into something rich and strange.

I could tell you about the world if it comes to that

That Sea nymphs ring his bell

where forests ancient as the hills,

Enfolding sunny spots of green

And gardens bright with sinuous rills,

blossom many an incense-bearing tree;

But I see panes of glass set back to back.

The Gates of Sense

Call it Fancy where the gates of sense are shut

and in their chambers

Sleep.

The Poisoned Ear

Murder moust foul as in the berst it is,
most foul, strange, and unnatural juice
of cursed plutonium
poured into the porches of the EAR (th).

The Alarm

Adam, Adam, Can you hear the alarm?

ADAM ADAM

The Angels of Orc

Fiery the Angels rose, and deep thunder roll'd

Around their shores

indignant fires burned with the flames of Orc.

The Death Trumpets

The trumpets sound.

Where had they been before

Death has always come for the world?

You know why we think

They sent the homeless in

to harness up and dive

the radioactive reef.

The Radioactive Reef

Boston, Seattle and LA were gone,

except for the eyes.

Tritium!

WHAT'S THAT?

Tritium! Tritium! Tritium!

The Elite Underground

Radiation burns atomic fuel.

The elite are going underground

The Path to North Canada

to be contaminated in their tombs.

The golden age sang merrily, along,

it sang—

Twice Five times of fertile ground

with walls and towers girdled round,

a perfect path to North Canada from Japan.

Everything long since d. and birds starved.

Bio-Magnification

As many atoms in one C137 gram

as in the world.

10 to the 21 bio-magnify the food chain up

with Berries and mushroom concentrate.

The Good News of 137

Good news 137

emits gamma radiation

to decay the number of Bq

per body weight sought-

The Curie and the Bq

One Curie means 37 billion atoms

disintegrating every second

One Bq is one decay per second.

Because these numbers are so large or small,

prefixes M or D make them readable

The Cesium Chair

In your Cesium chair

available from Steven Star.

The "Bq" of cesium depends upon on its mass.

Radioactive isotopes of cesium are extremely active compared

The Human Fire

A Human fire fierce glowing,

as the wedge of iron heated in the furnace;

his terrible limbs were fire.

The Geiger Counter

The becquerel only tells the rate of source.

It does not measure how much a body absorbs. Would you like to know how a Geiger counter turns these "decays" into a reading you can hear?

The Spectre glowed his horrid length
 the temple long
with beams of blood; & thus a voice came forth.

The Banana Click

click .click .. click . click . click ...click ...click .click ..went the banana

The Cesium Pop

cr-ck-ck-ck-ck-ck-ck-ck-ck-ck-rr-rr-rrrr-rrrrrrrrr went the Cesium 137 pops

Extreme wall

Saturation was a solid wall of

ZZZZZZZZZZZZZZZZZZZZZZZZZ

137 is a number numerologists can divine.

Compare the twicc five miles in Kubla Khan,

The worlds reflect their own strange fantasies.

A dragon form clashing his scales at midnight arose,

And flam'd red meteors round the land beneath His voice,

his locks, his awful shoulders, and his glowing eyes,

The real question comes if you go down the lane

hammering and break the panes.

Crash, bang, ca ching.

But watch your feet.

You won't believe.

Watch your feet,

watch your hands,

your eyes.

A virus can be multiplied.

And if the brain is blown to smithereens.

no krill, no urchins, no marine

And if a third part of the ocean died.

What's the cause of bird flu for?

Art thou not Orc, who serpent-form'd

Stands at the gate of Enitharmon

to devour her child?

Oh where

oh where

has the ice pack gone?

Fathom all the circles, pile stone,

each to each and the panes on either side,
It's nothing that you can't believe.

Why I believe it found out me!

You won't believe the birds went on a hunger strike
and died.
They ate too many bananas ripe.

Fires in-wrap the earthly globe,
yet man is not consumed;

Amidst the lustful fires he walks:
his feet become like brass,

His knees and thighs like silver,
& his breast and head like gold.
    And he's not that old!

He gloweth irradiant.

Must have flown too high --

got radiate at 40,000 feet.

His eyes have turned to pearls.

There's nothing left of him but eyes.

Geiger counter sales banned at 2020 Olympics!

Tokyo Olympians eat vegetables.

Except that sangine flower inscrib'd with woe,

Awoke that day and was exposed.

would none be saved.

He did not mask.

He would not mask.

No mask. Don't mask.

You ask. Don't mask,

Don’t mask don’t mask don’t mask don’t ask.

The daisies aren't deformers,
they're transformers. Facin-formed!

Sardines have Hormonal imbalance.
Snails random genetic disappearance.
And what about frog hermaphrodite
eggs from spontaneous temperature shifts in forested ponds. It isn’t
atrazine.
On Fiji, they died of heat stress.
Hong Kong fish farms fell in the red
TEPCO tide.

Some say it was brought by the boats.
We hope
Tasmanians got the POMS,
that Pacific Oyster Mortality Syndrome,

from their loose talk.

Shad in the Snake River got Exhausted
Fish Syndrome.

Japanese thyroid cancers up 6000%.
Molochs, Mollusks, daisies,
mutant rabbis put the K back in academe.

Sea nymphs ring his death bell every hour.

Fury! rage! madness in a wind swept through America
roaring fierce around the angry shores,
and the fierce rushing of the inhabitants together:

Citizens of New-York close
& lock their chests;
mariners of Boston drop,

their anchors unlade;

The scribe of Pennsylvania casts his pen

upon the earth;

The builder of Virginia throws his hammer down

Bacterial virials serve the banks in town.

Wm. Blake. America: A Prophecy

(1795)

Schools evacuate the faciation zone.

MOX mixed oxide fuel of Reactor 3 atomized aerosol.

On the head of a needle where Dr. Strangelove rode

the radioactive mind sprak 10,000 Bqs per foot.

Fiery the Angels rose,

& deep thunder roll'd around their shores:

indignant burning with the fires of Orc

Boston’s Angel cried aloud and flew

dark night.

The big advantage early in the event

besides not having as many lesions on your face

is you can say things true.

A lot like bagel, it don't prove much

if science got holes in its bagel pockets.

So many invites to extinction coming up

The states are zinging legal pot

that fat weed that roots itself in ease on Lethe's wharf,

It may look like bananas in a banana mine

where DARP and MITT copulate

in the banana clone

BED,

but the Banana Equivalent Dose of becquerel
Is only our second most exciting thrill
after food and sex,

To dose and show how little more you need

our BED,
our BED,
our BED

To murder you most foul
each hair will stand on end,

Bananas and potato chips give about the same
radioactive equivalence dose
to woop and worf all day

To breathe the sea-land transposition

A typical banana contains 15 Bq.

Their trucks alarms the entry ports

when passing through a Banana Radiation Monitor

—BAM—

A half gram of potassium velvet in the world

Fuk'ed to seventeen thousand a day,

skins and all brings

blinded Fury with the abhorred shears that slits

the TV set

all the way

to the ears.

Now take a razor blade and slit the eyeball screen

O wicked wit that has the power to seduce

to its shameful lust the will of my most seeming wit.

A single banana won't kill ya.

EVERYBODY DO THE FUKUSHIMA!

Give the homeless a free trip down,

 the disabled get equal opportunity by law.

If you ingest radioactive hebenon,

 you won’t be autoimmune for 15 years!

I got in trouble with the becquerel once

when Geoffrey Stanford at Greenhills had a spell:

he said,

"but who can see, who will hear

when we all slip on our bananna peel.

Bananas. And Daisies!

I can't make u-up my my-my-nde.

Bananna bananna bananna shorts.

Not to worry, fascine formed

Deformed

and fascinated dandelions

are not the lonesome all smooth bodies are.

--This is utterly without foundation and just disproves

the canceled out extinction of the Moon!

--Daisies "almost definitely"

are not radioactive mutants.

Daisy,

Daisy give me your answer do

TEPCO Organization for Deformed and Endangered Species

(TOES) formed in 1972

to plight the vanishing plant and man.

Which one are you?

Is where have all the flowers gone,

dandelions

fish

plankton

krill

anchovies

sardines

squid

herring

salmon,

mackerel

birds.

"The Fukushima plume is a good chance

to test radioactivity detection,"

Canada said.

One if by land,

Or by two!

The Pope built a wall,

the Giza Pyramid built a wall

Fukushima had its new wall back

And as we speak Dude,

fuel rods burn at 6000 to 9000 degrees!

Every atom belonging to you belongs to me!

We all gonna be one Fukushima!

We all gonna be one Fukushima!

When the morning comes.

Do the restoration more harm good.

Drop Cesium curds eager into milk.

Japan is going to be sent into the sun

with all the civilizations of the world.

If you want to know why goferments cover up the death of the

North Pacific

Stop.

Shut up!

It's not why, it’s not why, it’s not why.

it's not what, what, what or what.

Why o why o why-o

why o why o way

because because because

the great radioactive

glowworm shows the matin to be near,

no reckoning made.

Where were ye Nymphs when the remorseless deep

closed o'er my head?

These benzene drippings drip apart.

I thought the Japanese were smart.

They built the Toyota accelerator!

They built the fault lines.

They built near the sea.

They built tank farms on a hill

so drips could go down and melt,

and they built GE!

Tokyo Electric
built reactors as it did
so it would not pay the cost
if it blew a lid

Such effects as hold enmity with the blood of men
ate potassium iodide at Chernobyl and died
but those who ate sea kelp lived.

Reactor Three went down to China
On the Syndrome Train
so did One and Two.

A hundred tons melted in
liability corporate TV
Journalism schools ate the weapon,

Corporate Google GE

Nuke the nukes to personhood,

You won't be charged.

Corporate Radioactivity saves more lives

In spent fuel rods

Pool 4 at Fukushima went

Down swift Hebrus to the Lesbian shore.

I flown down that brandy cask for you sweet myrtles

in your ivy sere.

That cough's nothing.

It will not kill.

Ye shall not die of a cough!

electric! atomic

Whitman.

Poe.

The body,

The Body.

Like porcupine quills,

each fretful end to end.

Come pluck these berries harsh

and wear your thyroid crude.

Fukushima in 9 million one ton bags

made necklaces

for all communities round.

24 Empire State Buildings jumped to collect

USoma, Reactor 4

Before it saves the world.

ISIL! ISIl! on the wall!

Revelation again before.

First trump,

take her out and treat her like a lady.

Second trump,

tell her she's the one that you've been dreamin' of.

Third trump

take her in your arms and never let her go.

Don't you know that each half life is 4.2 billion years?

That's the way it goes.

Harrow soul, freeze blood,

two eyes start like stars from their spheres.

Somewhere Shakespeare Principalities
 blazon and fall.
Who's going to publish the news?
Murder-like Atoment.

The one too many world turn dreams
in the mist and the fogbound bush
alone in the violet forest hush
hurry up
 the coming rush of dreams is wished for in the light,
 dum-di-dum
the snake is squeezing
its eye is teasing
run snake run
dum-di-dum

the golden age of living

transplants is not yet out.

Oh Waltwald

My tongue, every atom of blood, Form'd

from this soil, this air, Born of parents here.

where each reactor holds 5 million lbs,

all melted down to thousands of cans

Blind Mouse,

Don’t drink. Don’t Drink, don’t drink.

that's the short list, oh!

Pity the H in fish.

Compare five miles girdled round

nine million bags of radioactive beer

compete with cocaine and antidepressants off the coast.

Young Chinnok in Puget Sound take H
 To slow them down.

MaryJane, Aleve and Tylenol.
Paxil, Valium, OxyContin,
 Darvon. Nicotine, caffeine, Cipro

Poet of Body and Soul,
how many Hiroshimas depend?

Flee you Vales,
or were you transhumized?

A thousand flee the valleys low.
Your emerald eyes throw Purple on the ground.

Fame as an infirmity in Chernobyl's mind.
Put put 50 Hiroshimas (H) Reactor 4
into mine air.

Japan will get a 10,
North America a 3
Europe a 1, according to Doc Jetstream.

Creeds in abeyance,
we got to fend for truth.

Make your reservations now for fairy tale.
go underground to know they want
to hire English teachers down.

Yale is going to Denver,

so no worry, get your degree.

They go to work in the mortgage fields below,

where Dante works the lame,

halt and blind

scramble at the shearers feast.

Experts by dozens are never wrong.

Detonations, explosions, releases

Grate on your scrannel pipes of straw.

Is this the second Seal or 6th?

Wormwood thought

it was Chernobyl when it fell

but 50 times Hiroshima guy can't speak.

Wildlife extinction has been achieved.

Here was once the laureate hearse of Lycidas'

gory vis-age.

He did get cancer results from all the nuclear Homeland tests,

To comfort the sacrosanct in this:

Each reactor had 3450 assemblies.

Each assembly had 80 rods.

Each rod had 18 lbs.

so each reactor had 5 million pounds.

It's laying like an egg.

Chernobyl's equivalent of 400 Hiroshima bomb 10 days.

Fukushima has 500,000 bombs, so far.

Look homeward angel now and melt.

Its name is written on the forehead of its

Bellowing

that all myths are public dreams,

and dreams

are private myths that stuff

collective unLoosed.

Who you think invented nuclear power, fallen troops?

Sometimes angels,

sometimes devils.

Hig a pig a pop,

Anaxagoras IAEA exposed all his rods.

Lust to a radiant angel linked, will sate itself.

TEPCO is calling.

The meditation pools are leaking.

Six li'l reactors

was sittin' in lead,

Three was sick
so the other ones said.

Send for the doctor,
and the doctor said,
get them little meltdowns
some absorption lead.

Tepco's little baby
had a meltdown meltdown
Tepco's little baby
on a meltdown sped.

I write to you Krypton 85 to make California safe.
I write to you horticultural Cesium
to break out strontium tares,
Out of it make smores.

I drink you Tokoy water with BAM Iodine-131.

Bring your 30 million Bq/mz soil mix.

We shall grow a radish.

Deformed daises bring your bow,

bring me your bananas of desire!

Daisy daisy give me your answer do.

Our Hormesis hypothesis is this

-----to cure strontium eat spinach.

In converse get chemotherapy

Sign a waiver.

Experiment your own genes

and 90% children!

Tritium,

strontium 90,

Iodine 131,

Cesium 137

trace 2000 madman elements classified

If all the tracers present in reaction chains

in this snowstorm time

you can't see or feel,

shovel fast, its 15 million year half/life

will outlast

the beaks off Promontory.

If you're a journalist in Japan

report the rapes in France.

Outraged animal carcasses

litter the Fukushima plant.

Billions of baby blue jellyfish "driven by the wind"
Settle on the beaches of Canada and Oregano.

They must not float upon the watery bier Unwept,
and welter to the parching wind.

We're not supposed to say it.
We're not supposed to say it.
Three million children got disabilities at Chernobyl.

Worried about snow melt?
Man, Tritium prevents ice crystal not the sun
who tricks his beams with this new-spangled Ore.

Atoms bio-accumulate immune,
deficiencies spread.
Cancer with parasites,
pathogens prep the body ph electric

Virus Pulse each second, "the wasting disease."

The Longest Poem Ever Wrote

now leads Finland to its briny waste,

250,000 tons of high grade stuff,

100,000 years of sleep remain in rock.

The Finns took 1700 feet down to BED the banana!

Bedrock 1.8 billion years would take

the fire to not put out,

stuck down like a treasure not to be found.

like ocean pyramids

Secret societies of doubt

Nuke it out,

It leaves a jar of liver paste

To mark the site

At Onkalo and its spent fuel rods.

This writing see:

Mark but this flea!

It sucked me first,

and now sucks thee,

And cloistered in these walls of jet.

Let not to that, self-murder added be,

Though use make you apt to kill me,

Let not to that, self-murder added be.

That Donne marker

left a feeling of thorns

so one, ever goes

LOOking

To put fire on top the ground so anyone

who dies

Has to dig death not to survive.

I'll wipe away all trivial fond records, all saws of books,

all forms that youth and observation copied there

and this commandment alone shall give:

RUN!

Satan inorganic.

Giza's death ray,

  fire put to sleep,

 never remember thee.

Remember to remember to forever forget.

They worry about the future who made it what it is,

They sock the hole they stop.

This is the law.

Black metal updates

archive language at each predicted thaw.

Legends whose secret vaults

Worldwide.

Worse than any who ever lived,

repudiate the greed of radioactivity.

Greater deformity each succeeding gen,

2 worse than 1, three worse than two.

Cicadas, butterflies, pink grasshoppers,

Kodiak bears with holes

in their hearts,

Chernobyl heart children with 20-30 Bq/kg Cesium

heart defects.

Japan heart attacks in youth

Are caused by too much fast food!

Five billion Strontium 90 Bq

goes in the sea EACH DAY.

The perps are planning to fumigate to Mars

Notes

Page 1: "Six li'l reactors..."

The opening sequence parodies the traditional children's fingerplay and counting rhyme "Five Little Monkeys Jumping on the Bed," reframed here to address the six reactor units at the Fukushima Daiichi Nuclear Power Plant.

Page 2: "Radiation flows from them like an issue of blood."

An allusion to the biblical account of the woman with the "issue of blood" found in **Mark 5:25–34**.

Page 3: "He's undergone a complete sea change..."

The lines "into something rich and strange" and "Sea nymphs ring his bell" are taken from Ariel's Song in **William Shakespeare's *The Tempest*** (Act I, Scene II).

Page 3: "where forests ancient as the hills..."

Lines beginning here through "incense-bearing tree" are sourced from **Samuel Taylor Coleridge's "Kubla Khan"** (1816).

Page 4: "Murder most foul..."

Direct quotation from **William Shakespeare's *Hamlet*** (Act I, Scene V), specifically the Ghost's revelation to Hamlet regarding his "strange and unnatural" murder. The substitution of "plutonium" for "hebenon" serves as a contemporary ecopoetic update.

Page 5: "Fiery the Angels rose..."

This section incorporates lines and imagery from **William Blake's *America: A Prophecy*** (1793), specifically regarding the character Orc, who symbolizes revolutionary spirit and "indignant fires."

Page 7: "137 emits gamma radiation..."

Refers to **Cesium-137**, a radioactive isotope produced by nuclear fission. The "Bq" refers to the **Becquerel**, the SI derived unit of radioactivity, defined as the activity of a quantity of radioactive material in which one nucleus decays per second.

Page 8: "One Curie means 37 billion atoms..."

The **Curie (Ci)** is a non-SI unit of radioactivity originally defined in 1910. The text contrasts the macro-scale of the Curie with the micro-scale of the Becquerel.

Page 9: "The Spectre glowed his horrid length..."

This imagery and phrasing are drawn from **William Blake's *The Four Zoas*** and his broader mythological framework regarding the "Spectre" as a shadow of the rational man.

Page 20: "Banana Equivalent Dose (BED)..."

The BED is an informal measurement of ionizing radiation exposure, intended as a general educational example to compare a dose of radioactivity to that eaten in one average-sized banana.

27.
28. **Page 1: Title Page** (Title only: *The Annotated History of the World*)
29. **Page 2: Table of Contents**
30. **Page 3: I. Six Li'l Reactors** (Break after "...six nukes.")
31. **Page 4: The Nuke Family** (Break after "What's wrong with him?")
32. **Page 5: The Sea Change** (Break after "set back to back.")
33. **Page 6: The Gates of Sense** (Break after "Sleep.")
34. **Page 7: The Poisoned Ear** (Break after "porches of the EAR (th).")
35. **Page 8: The Alarm** (Break after the second "ADAM ADAM")
36. **Page 9: The Angels of Orc** (Break after "flames of Orc.")
37. **Page 10: The Death Trumpets** (Break after "harness up and dive")
38. **Page 11: The Radioactive Reef** (Break after "except for the eyes.")
39. **Page 12: Tritium!** (Break after "Tritium! Tritium! Tritium!")
40. **Page 13: The Elite Underground** (Break after "contaminated in their tombs.")
41. **Page 14: The Path to North Canada** (Break after "Everything long since d. and birds starved.")
42. **Page 15: Bio-Magnification** (Break after "mushroom concentrate.")
43. **Page 16: The Good News of 137** (Break after "Bq per body weight sought-")
44. **Page 17: The Curie and the Bq** (Break after "make them readable")
45. **Page 18: The Cesium Chair** (Break after "Radioactive isotopes of cesium are extremely active compared")

46. **Page 19: The Human Fire** (Break after "limbs were fire.")
47. **Page 20: The Geiger Counter** (Break after "reading you can hear?")
48. **Page 21: The Spectre's Voice** (Break after "a voice came forth.")
49. **Page 22: The Banana Click** (Break after "went the banana")
50. **Page 23: The Cesium Pop** (Break after "went the Cesium 137 pops")
51. **Page 24: Extreme Saturation** (Break after the "ZZZZZZZZZZ" wall)
52. **Page 25: The Numerology of 137** (Break after "Kubla Khan,")
53. **Page 26: The Dragon Arises** (Break after "at midnight arose,")

The Annotated History of the World

Table of Contents

II. Six Li'l Reactors

Six li'l reactors

Was sittin' in lead,

Three got sick

so the other ones went,

They sent for the doctor,

but the doctor said,

get them little meltdowns

some explosion bread.

Tepco's little baby

had a meltdown meltdown

Tepco's little baby

on a meltdown sped.

The Nuke Family

Once upon a time there were six nukes.

A momma nuke, a poppa nuke and a MOX nuke baby who lost

their cores in earth.

Who's been stealing my core, said number four?

Who knows where they are?

Radiation flows from them like an issue of blood.

The north Pacific beyond is the woman of EARth

Tritium!

Tritium!

What's wrong with him?

The Sea Change

He's undergone a complete sea change

into something rich and strange.

I could tell you about the world if it comes to that

That Sea nymphs ring his bell

where forests ancient as the hills,

Enfolding sunny spots of green

And gardens bright with sinuous rills,

blossom many an incense-bearing tree;

But I see panes of glass set back to back.

The Gates of Sense

Call it Fancy where the gates of sense are shut

and in their chambers

Sleep.

The Poisoned Ear

Murder moust foul as in the berst it is,

most foul, strange, and unnatural juice

of cursed plutonium

poured into the porches of the EAR (th).

The Alarm

Adam, Adam, Can you hear the alarm?

ADAM ADAM

The Angels of Orc

Fiery the Angels rose, and deep thunder roll'd

Around their shores

indignant fires burned with the flames of Orc.

The Death Trumpets

The trumpets sound.

Where had they been before

Death has always come for the world?

You know why we think

They sent the homeless in

to harness up and dive

the radioactive reef.

The Radioactive Reef

Boston, Seattle and LA were gone,

except for the eyes.

Tritium!

WHAT'S THAT?

Tritium! Tritium! Tritium!

The Elite Underground

Radiation burns atomic fuel.

The elite are going underground

The Path to North Canada

to be contaminated in their tombs.

The golden age sang merrily, along,

it sang—

Twice Five times of fertile ground

with walls and towers girdled round,

a perfect path to North Canada from Japan.

Everything long since d. and birds starved.

Bio-Magnification

As many atoms in one C137 gram

as in the world.

10 to the 21 bio-magnify the food chain up

with Berries and mushroom concentrate.

The Good News of 137

Good news 137

emits gamma radiation

to decay the number of Bq

per body weight sought-

The Curie and the Bq

One Curie means 37 billion atoms

disintegrating every second

One Bq is one decay per second.

Because these numbers are so large or small,

prefixes M or D make them readable

The Cesium Chair

In your Cesium chair

available from Steven Star.

The "Bq" of cesium depends upon on its mass.

Radioactive isotopes of cesium are extremely active compared

The Human Fire

A Human fire fierce glowing,

as the wedge of iron heated in the furnace;

his terrible limbs were fire.

The Geiger Counter

The becquerel only tells the rate of source.

It does not measure how much a body absorbs. Would you like to know how a Geiger counter turns these "decays" into a reading you can hear?

The Spectre's Voice

The Spectre glowed his horrid length

the temple long

with beams of blood; & thus a voice came forth.

The Banana Click

click .click .. click . click . click ...click ...click .click ..went the banana

The Cesium Pop

cr-ck-ck-ck-ck-ck-ck-ck-ck-ck-rr-rr-rrrr-rrrrrrrrr went the Cesium 137 pops

Extreme wall

Saturation was a solid wall of
ZZZZZZZZZZZZZZZZZZZZZZZZZZ

137 is a number numerologists can divine.
Compare the twice five miles in Kubla Khan,
The worlds reflect their own strange fantasies.
A dragon form clashing his scales at midnight arose,
And flam'd red meteors round the land beneath His voice,
his locks, his awful shoulders, and his glowing eyes,
The real question comes if you go down the lane
hammering and break the panes.

Crash, bang, ca ching.
But watch your feet.
You won't believe.

Watch your feet,
watch your hands,

your eyes.

A virus can be multiplied.

And if the brain is blown to smithereens.

no krill, no urchins, no marine

And if a third part of the ocean died.

What's the cause of bird flu for?

Art thou not Orc, who serpent-form'd

Stands at the gate of Enitharmon

to devour her child?

Oh where

oh where

has the ice pack gone?

Fathom all the circles, pile stone,

each to each and the panes on either side,

It's nothing that you can’t believe.

Why I believe it found out me!

You won't believe the birds went on a hunger strike
and died.
They ate too many bananas ripe.

Fires in-wrap the earthly globe,
yet man is not consumed;

Amidst the lustful fires he walks:
his feet become like brass,

His knees and thighs like silver,
& his breast and head like gold.
And he’s not that old!

He gloweth irradiant.

Must have flown too high --

got radiate at 40,000 feet.

His eyes have turned to pearls.

There's nothing left of him but eyes.

Geiger counter sales banned at 2020 Olympics!

Tokyo Olympians eat vegetables.

Except that sangine flower inscrib'd with woe,

Awoke that day and was exposed.

would none be saved.

He did not mask.

He would not mask.

No mask. Don't mask.

You ask. Don't mask,

Don't mask don't mask don't mask don't ask.

The daisies aren't deformers,
they're transformers. Facin-formed!

Sardines have Hormonal imbalance.
Snails random genetic disappearance.
And what about frog hermaphrodite
eggs from spontaneous temperature shifts in forested ponds. It isn’t
atrazine.
On Fiji, they died of heat stress.
Hong Kong fish farms fell in the red
TEPCO tide.

Some say it was brought by the boats.
We hope
Tasmanians got the POMS,
that Pacific Oyster Mortality Syndrome,
from their loose talk.

Shad in the Snake River got Exhausted
Fish Syndrome.

Japanese thyroid cancers up 6000%.
Molochs, Mollusks, daisies,
mutant rabbis put the K back in academe.

Sea nymphs ring his death bell every hour.

Fury! rage! madness in a wind swept through America
roaring fierce around the angry shores,
and the fierce rushing of the inhabitants together:

Citizens of New-York close
& lock their chests;
mariners of Boston drop,
their anchors unlade;

The scribe of Pennsylvania casts his pen

upon the earth;

The builder of Virginia throws his hammer down

Bacterial virials serve the banks in town.

Wm. Blake. America: A Prophecy

(1795)

Schools evacuate the faciation zone.

MOX mixed oxide fuel of Reactor 3 atomized aerosol.

On the head of a needle where Dr. Strangelove rode

the radioactive mind sprak 10,000 Bqs per foot.

Fiery the Angels rose,

& deep thunder roll'd around their shores:

indignant burning with the fires of Orc

Boston's Angel cried aloud and flew
dark night.

The big advantage early in the event
besides not having as many lesions on your face
is you can say things true.

A lot like bagel, it don't prove much
if science got holes in its bagel pockets.

So many invites to extinction coming up
The states are zinging legal pot
that fat weed that roots itself in ease on Lethe's wharf,
It may look like bananas in a banana mine
where DARP and MITT copulate
in the banana clone
BED,

but the Banana Equivalent Dose of becquerel
Is only our second most exciting thrill
after food and sex,

To dose and show how little more you need

our BED,
our BED,
our BED

To murder you most foul
each hair will stand on end,

Bananas and potato chips give about the same
radioactive equivalence dose
to woop and worf all day

To breathe the sea-land transposition

A typical banana contains 15 Bq.

Their trucks alarms the entry ports

when passing through a Banana Radiation Monitor

—BAM—

A half gram of potassium velvet in the world

Fuk'ed to seventeen thousand a day,

skins and all brings

blinded Fury with the abhorred shears that slits

the TV set

all the way

to the ears.

Now take a razor blade and slit the eyeball screen

O wicked wit that has the power to seduce

to its shameful lust the will of my most seeming wit.

A single banana won't kill ya.

EVERYBODY DO THE FUKUSHIMA!

Give the homeless a free trip down,

the disabled get equal opportunity by law.

If you ingest radioactive hebenon,

you won’t be autoimmune for 15 years!

I got in trouble with the becquerel once

when Geoffrey Stanford at Greenhills had a spell:

he said,

"but who can see, who will hear

when we all slip on our bananna peel.

Bananas. And Daisies!

I can't make u-up my my-my-nde.

Bananna bananna bananna shorts.

Not to worry, fascine formed

Deformed

and fascinated dandelions

are not the lonesome all smooth bodies are.

--This is utterly without foundation and just disproves

the canceled out extinction of the Moon!

--Daisies "almost definitely"

are not radioactive mutants.

Daisy,

Daisy give me your answer do

TEPCO Organization for Deformed and Endangered Species

(TOES) formed in 1972

to plight the vanishing plant and man.

Which one are you?

Is where have all the flowers gone,

dandelions

fish

plankton

krill

anchovies

sardines

squid

herring

salmon,

mackerel

birds.

"The Fukushima plume is a good chance

to test radioactivity detection,"

Canada said.

One if by land,

Or by two!

The Pope built a wall,

the Giza Pyramid built a wall

Fukushima had its new wall back

And as we speak Dude,

fuel rods burn at 6000 to 9000 degrees!

Every atom belonging to you belongs to me!

We all gonna be one Fukushima!

We all gonna be one Fukushima!

When the morning comes.

Do the restoration more harm good.

Drop Cesium curds eager into milk.

Japan is going to be sent into the sun

with all the civilizations of the world.

If you want to know why goferments cover up the death of the

North Pacific

Stop.

Shut up!

It's not why, it’s not why, it’s not why.

it's not what, what, what or what.

Why o why o why-o

why o why o way

because because because

the great radioactive

glowworm shows the matin to be near,

no reckoning made.

Where were ye Nymphs when the remorseless deep

closed o'er my head?

These benzene drippings drip apart.

I thought the Japanese were smart.

They built the Toyota accelerator!

They built the fault lines.

They built near the sea.

They built tank farms on a hill

so drips could go down and melt,

and they built GE!

Tokyo Electric

built reactors as it did

so it would not pay the cost

if it blew a lid

Such effects as hold enmity with the blood of men

ate potassium iodide at Chernobyl and died

but those who ate sea kelp lived.

Reactor Three went down to China

On the Syndrome Train

so did One and Two.

A hundred tons melted in

liability corporate TV

Journalism schools ate the weapon,

Corporate Google GE

Nuke the nukes to personhood,

You won't be charged.

Corporate Radioactivity saves more lives

In spent fuel rods

Pool 4 at Fukushima went

Down swift Hebrus to the Lesbian shore.

I flown down that brandy cask for you sweet myrtles

in your ivy sere.

That cough's nothing.

It will not kill.

Ye shall not die of a cough!

electric! atomic

Whitman.

Poe.

The body,

The Body.

Like porcupine quills,

each fretful end to end.

Come pluck these berries harsh

and wear your thyroid crude.

Fukushima in 9 million one ton bags

made necklaces

for all communities round.

24 Empire State Buildings jumped to collect

USoma, Reactor 4

Before it saves the world.

ISIL! ISIl! on the wall!

Revelation again before.

First trump,

take her out and treat her like a lady.

Second trump,

tell her she's the one that you've been dreamin' of.

Third trump

take her in your arms and never let her go.

Don't you know that each half life is 4.2 billion years?

That's the way it goes.

Harrow soul, freeze blood,

two eyes start like stars from their spheres.

Somewhere Shakespeare Principalities

blazon and fall.

Who's going to publish the news?

Murder-like Atoment.

The one too many world turn dreams

in the mist and the fogbound bush

alone in the violet forest hush

hurry up

the coming rush of dreams is wished for in the light,

dum-di-dum

the snake is squeezing

its eye is teasing

run snake run

dum-di-dum

the golden age of living

transplants is not yet out.

Oh Waltwald

My tongue, every atom of blood, Form'd
from this soil, this air, Born of parents here.
where each reactor holds 5 million lbs,
all melted down to thousands of cans

Blind Mouse,
Don’t drink. Don’t Drink, don’t drink.

that's the short list, oh!
Pity the H in fish.

Compare five miles girdled round
nine million bags of radioactive beer

compete with cocaine and antidepressants off the coast.

Young Chinnok in Puget Sound take H

To slow them down.

MaryJane, Aleve and Tylenol.

Paxil, Valium, OxyContin,

Darvon. Nicotine, caffeine, Cipro

Poet of Body and Soul,

how many Hiroshimas depend?

Flee you Vales,

or were you transhumized?

A thousand flee the valleys low.

Your emerald eyes throw Purple on the ground.

Fame as an infirmity in Chernobyl's mind.

Put put 50 Hiroshimas (H) Reactor 4

into mine air.

Japan will get a 10,

North America a 3

Europe a 1, according to Doc Jetstream.

Creeds in abeyance,

we got to fend for truth.

Make your reservations now for fairy tale.

go underground to know they want

to hire English teachers down.

Yale is going to Denver,

so no worry, get your degree.

They go to work in the mortgage fields below,

where Dante works the lame,
halt and blind
scramble at the shearers feast.

Experts by dozens are never wrong.
Detonations, explosions, releases
Grate on your scrannel pipes of straw.
Is this the second Seal or 6th?

Wormwood thought
it was Chernobyl when it fell
but 50 times Hiroshima guy can't speak.

Wildlife extinction has been achieved.

Here was once the laureate hearse of Lycidas'

gory vis-age.

He did get cancer results from all the nuclear Homeland tests,

To comfort the sacrosanct in this:

Each reactor had 3450 assemblies.

Each assembly had 80 rods.

Each rod had 18 lbs.

so each reactor had 5 million pounds.

It's laying like an egg.

Chernobyl's equivalent of 400 Hiroshima bomb 10 days.

Fukushima has 500,000 bombs, so far.

Look homeward angel now and melt.

Its name is written on the forehead of its

Bellowing

that all myths are public dreams,

and dreams

are private myths that stuff

collective unLoosed.

Who you think invented nuclear power, fallen troops?

Sometimes angels,

sometimes devils.

Hig a pig a pop,

Anaxagoras IAEA exposed all his rods.

Lust to a radiant angel linked, will sate itself.

TEPCO is calling.

The meditation pools are leaking.

Six li'l reactors

was sittin' in lead,

Three was sick

so the other ones said.

Send for the doctor,

and the doctor said,

get them little meltdowns

some absorption lead.

Tepco's little baby

had a meltdown meltdown

Tepco's little baby

on a meltdown sped.

I write to you Krypton 85 to make California safe.

I write to you horticultural Cesium

to break out strontium tares,

Out of it make smores.

I drink you Tokoy water with BAM Iodine-131.

Bring your 30 million Bq/mz soil mix.

We shall grow a radish.

Deformed daises bring your bow,

bring me your bananas of desire!

Daisy daisy give me your answer do.

Our Hormesis hypothesis is this

-----to cure strontium eat spinach.

In converse get chemotherapy

Sign a waiver.

Experiment your own genes

and 90% children!

Tritium,

strontium 90,

Iodine 131,

Cesium 137

trace 2000 madman elements classified

If all the tracers present in reaction chains

in this snowstorm time

you can't see or feel,

shovel fast, its 15 million year half/life

will outlast

the beaks off Promontory.

If you're a journalist in Japan

report the rapes in France.

Outraged animal carcasses

 litter the Fukushima plant.

Billions of baby blue jellyfish "driven by the wind"

Settle on the beaches of Canada and Oregano.

They must not float upon the watery bier Unwept,

and welter to the parching wind.

We're not supposed to say it.

We're not supposed to say it.

Three million children got disabilities at Chernobyl.

Worried about snow melt?

Man, Tritium prevents ice crystal not the sun

who tricks his beams with this new-spangled Ore.

Atoms bio-accumulate immune,

deficiencies spread.

Cancer with parasites,

pathogens prep the body ph electric

Virus Pulse each second, "the wasting disease."

The Longest Poem Ever Wrote

now leads Finland to its briny waste,

250,000 tons of high grade stuff,
100,000 years of sleep remain in rock.
The Finns took 1700 feet down to BED the banana!

Bedrock 1.8 billion years would take
the fire to not put out,
stuck down like a treasure not to be found.

like ocean pyramids
Secret societies of doubt
Nuke it out,
It leaves a jar of liver paste
To mark the site
At Onkalo and its spent fuel rods.

This writing see:

Mark but this flea!

It sucked me first,

and now sucks thee,

And cloistered in these walls of jet.

Let not to that, self-murder added be,

Though use make you apt to kill me,

Let not to that, self-murder added be.

That Donne marker

left a feeling of thorns

so one, ever goes

LOOking

To put fire on top the ground so anyone

who dies

Has to dig death not to survive.

I'll wipe away all trivial fond records, all saws of books,
all forms that youth and observation copied there
and this commandment alone shall give:

RUN!
Satan inorganic.
Giza's death ray,
  fire put to sleep,
 never remember thee.

Remember to remember to forever forget.

They worry about the future who made it what it is,

They sock the hole they stop.

This is the law.

Black metal updates

archive language at each predicted thaw.

Legends whose secret vaults

Worldwide.

Worse than any who ever lived,

repudiate the greed of radioactivity.

Greater deformity each succeeding gen,

2 worse than 1, three worse than two.

Cicadas, butterflies, pink grasshoppers,

Kodiak bears with holes

in their hearts,

Chernobyl heart children with 20-30 Bq/kg Cesium

heart defects.

Japan heart attacks in youth

Are caused by too much fast food!

Five billion Strontium 90 Bq

goes in the sea EACH DAY.

The perps are planning to fumigate to Mars

Notes

Page 1: "Six li'l reactors..."

The opening sequence parodies the traditional children's fingerplay and counting rhyme "Five Little Monkeys Jumping on the Bed," reframed here to address the six reactor units at the Fukushima Daiichi Nuclear Power Plant.

Page 2: "Radiation flows from them like an issue of blood."

An allusion to the biblical account of the woman with the "issue of blood" found in **Mark 5:25–34**.

Page 3: "He's undergone a complete sea change..."

The lines "into something rich and strange" and "Sea nymphs ring his bell" are taken from Ariel's Song in **William Shakespeare's *The Tempest*** (Act I, Scene II).

Page 3: "where forests ancient as the hills..."

Lines beginning here through "incense-bearing tree" are sourced from **Samuel Taylor Coleridge's "Kubla Khan"** (1816).

Page 4: "Murder most foul..."

Direct quotation from **William Shakespeare's *Hamlet*** (Act I, Scene V), specifically the Ghost's revelation to Hamlet regarding his "strange and unnatural" murder. The substitution of "plutonium" for "hebenon" serves as a contemporary ecopoetic update.

Page 5: "Fiery the Angels rose..."

This section incorporates lines and imagery from **William Blake's *America: A Prophecy*** (1793), specifically regarding the character Orc, who symbolizes revolutionary spirit and "indignant fires."

Page 7: "137 emits gamma radiation..."

Refers to **Cesium-137**, a radioactive isotope produced by nuclear fission. The "Bq" refers to the **Becquerel**, the SI derived unit of radioactivity, defined as the activity of a quantity of radioactive material in which one nucleus decays per second.

Page 8: "One Curie means 37 billion atoms..."

The **Curie (Ci)** is a non-SI unit of radioactivity originally defined in 1910. The text contrasts the macro-scale of the Curie with the micro-scale of the Becquerel.

Page 9: "The Spectre glowed his horrid length..."

This imagery and phrasing are drawn from **William Blake's *The Four Zoas*** and his broader mythological framework regarding the "Spectre" as a shadow of the rational man.

Page 20: "Banana Equivalent Dose (BED)..."

The BED is an informal measurement of ionizing radiation exposure, intended as a general educational example to compare a dose of radioactivity to that eaten in one average-sized banana.

The Jolly Rubino

Six li'l reactors
Was sittin' in lead,
Three got sick
so the other ones went,

They sent for the doctor,
but the doctor said,
get them little meltdowns
some explosion bread.

Tepco's little baby
had a meltdown meltdown
Tepco's little baby
on a meltdown sped.

The Jolly Rubino

Once upon a time there were six nukes.
A momma nuke, a poppa nuke and a MOX nuke
baby
who lost their cores in earth.

Who's been stealing my core, said number four?
Who knows where they are?

Radiation flows from them like an issue of blood.
The north Pacific beyond is the woman of earth

Tritium!
Tritium!

What's wrong with him?

He's undergone a complete sea change
into something rich and strange.

I could tell you about the world if it comes to that

That Sea nymphs ring his bell

where forests ancient as the hills,

Enfolding sunny spots of green

And gardens bright with sinuous rills,

blossom many an incense-bearing tree;

But I see panes of glass set back to back.

Call it Fancy where the gates of sense are shut

and in their chambers

Sleep.

Murder moust foul as in the berst it is,

most foul, Hamlet, Act I, Scene V

strange, and unnatural juice of cursed plutonium

poured

into the porches of the EAR (th).

*

Adam, Adam, Can you hear the alarm?

ADAM ADAM

*

Fiery the Angels rose, and deep thunder roll'd
Around their shores
indignant fires burned with the flames of Orc.

The trumpets sound.
Where had they been before
Death has always come for the world?

You know why we think
They sent the homeless in
to harness up and dive
the radioactive reef.

Boston, Seattle and LA were gone,

except for the eyes.

WHAT'S THAT?

Tritium! Tritium! Tritium!

Radiation burns atomic fuel.
The elite are going underground
to be contaminated in their tombs.

The golden age sang merrily, along,
it sang—

Twice Five times of fertile ground
with walls and towers girdled round,

a perfect path to North Canada from Japan.
Everything long since d. and birds starved.

As many atoms in one C137 gram
as in the world.

10 to the 21 bio-magnify the food chain up

with Berries and mushroom concentrate.

Good news 137
emits gamma radiation
to decay the number of Bq

per body weight sought-

One Curie means **37 billion atoms**
disintegrating every second
One Bq is **one decay per second**.
Because these numbers are so large or small,
prefixes M or D make them readable

In your Cesium chair

available from Steven Star.

The "Bq" of cesium depends upon on its mass.
Radioactive isotopes of cesium are extremely active compared

A Human fire fierce glowing,

as the wedge of iron heated in the furnace;

his terrible limbs were fire.

**The becquerel only tells the rate of the source.
It does not measure how much radiation a body absorbs.
Would you like to know how a Geiger counter turns these "decays" into a reading you can hear?**

The Spectre glowed his horrid length the temple long

with beams of blood; & thus a voice came forth.

click .click .. click . click . click ...click ...click .click ..went the banana

cr-ck-ck-ck-ck-ck-ck-ck-ck-ck-rr-rr-rrrr-rrrrrrrrr went the Cesium 137 pops

Extreme Saturation was a solid wall of
ZZZZZZZZZZZZZZZZZZZZZZZZZ

137 is a number numerologists can divine.
Compare the twice five miles in Kubla Khan,
The worlds reflect their own strange fantasies.

A dragon form clashing his scales at midnight arose,

And flam'd red meteors round the land beneath His voice,

his locks, his awful shoulders, and his glowing
eyes,

The real question comes if you go down the
lane
hammering and break the panes.

Crash, bang, ca
ching.
But watch your feet.
You won't believe.

Watch your feet,
watch your hands,
your eyes.
A virus can be multiplied.

And if the brain is blown to smithereens.

no krill, no urchins, no marine

And if a third part of the ocean died.
What's the cause of bird flu for?

Art thou not Orc, who serpent-form'd
Stands at the gate of Enitharmon
to devour her child?

Oh where
oh where
has the ice pack gone?
Fathom all the circles, pile stone,
each to each and the panes on either side,
It's nothing that you can't believe.

Why I believe it found out me!

You won't believe the birds went on a
hunger strike
and died.
They ate too many bananas ripe.

Fires in-wrap the earthly globe,
yet man is not consumed;

Amidst the lustful fires he walks:
his feet become like brass,

His knees and thighs like silver,
& his breast and head like gold.
And he's not that old!

He gloweth irradiant.

Must have flown too high --

got radiate at 40,000 feet.

His eyes have turned to pearls.

There's nothing left of him but eyes.

Geiger counter sales banned at 2020

Olympics!

Tokyo Olympians eat vegetables.

Except that sangine flower inscrib'd with woe,

Awoke that day and was exposed.

would none be saved.

He did not mask.

He would not mask.

No mask. Don't mask.

You ask. Don't mask,

Don't mask don't mask don't mask
don't ask.

The daisies aren't deformers,
they're transformers. **Facin-formed**!

Sardines have Hormonal imbalance.
Snails random genetic disappearance.
And what about frog hermaphrodite
eggs from spontaneous temperature shifts in
forested ponds. It isn't atrazine.
On Fiji, they died of heat stress.
Hong Kong fish farms fell in the red
TEPCO tide.

Some say it was brought by the
boats.

We hope

Tasmanians got the POMS,
that **P**acific **O**yster **M**ortality
Syndrome,
from their loose talk.

Shad in the Snake River got
Exhausted
Fish Syndrome.

Japanese thyroid cancers up 6000%.
Molochs, Mollusks, daisies,
mutant rabbis put the K back in
academe.

Sea nymphs ring his death bell every hour.

Fury! rage! madness in *a wind swept*
through America
roaring fierce around the angry shores,
and the fierce rushing of the inhabitants
together:

Citizens of New-York close
& lock their chests;
mariners of Boston drop,
their anchors unlade;

The scribe of Pennsylvania casts his pen
upon the earth;

The builder of Virginia throws his hammer
down

Bacterial virials serve the banks *in town.*

Wm. Blake. America: A Prophecy (1795)

Schools evacuate the faciation zone.
MOX mixed oxide fuel of Reactor 3 atomized aerosol.

On the head of a needle where Dr. Strangelove rode
the radioactive mind sprak 10,000 Bqs per foot.

Fiery the Angels rose,

& deep thunder roll'd around their shores:

indignant burning with the fires of Orc

Boston's Angel cried aloud and flew

dark night.

The big advantage early in the
event
besides not having as many lesions on your
face
is you can say things true.

A lot like bagel, it don't prove much
if science got holes in its bagel pockets.

So many invites to extinction coming up
The states are zinging legal
pot

that fat weed that roots itself in ease on Lethe's wharf,

It may look like bananas in a banana mine
where DARP and MITT copulate
in the banana clone
BED,

but the **Banana Equivalent Dose** of
becquerel
Is only our second most exciting thrill
after food and sex,

To dose and show how little more you need

our BED,
our BED,
our BED

To murder you most foul
each hair will stand on end,

Bananas and potato chips give
about the same
radioactive equivalence dose
to woop and worf all day

To breathe the sea-land
transposition
A typical banana contains 15 Bq.

Their trucks alarms the entry ports
when passing through a Banana
Radiation Monitor

—BAM—

A half gram of potassium velvet in
the world
Fuk'ed to seventeen thousand a day,
skins and all brings

blinded Fury with the abhorred shears that
slits

the TV set
all the way
to the ears.

Now take a razor blade and slit the eyeball
screen

O wicked wit that has the power to seduce

to its shameful lust the will of my most seeming wit.

A single banana won't kill ya.

EVERYBODY DO THE FUKUSHIMA!

Give the homeless a free trip down,
the disabled get equal opportunity by law.

If you ingest radioactive hebenon,
you won't be autoimmune for 15 years!

I got in trouble with the becquerel once
when Geoffrey Stanford at Greenhills had a spell:

he said,

"but who can see, who will hear
when we all slip on our bananna peel.

Bananas. And Daisies!
I can't make u-up my my-my-nde.

Bananna bananna bananna shorts.

Not to worry, fascine formed
Deformed
and fascinated dandelions
are not the lonesome all smooth bodies are.

--This is utterly without foundation and just
disproves
the canceled out extinction of the Moon!

--Daisies "almost definitely"
are not radioactive mutants.

Daisy,
Daisy give me your answer do

TEPCO Organization for Deformed and
Endangered Species
(TOES) formed in 1972

to plight the vanishing plant and man.
Which one are you?

Is where have all the flowers gone,

dandelions

fish

plankton

krill

anchovies

sardines

squid

herring

salmon,

mackerel

birds.

"The Fukushima plume is a good chance

to test radioactivity detection,"

Canada said.

One if by land,

Or by two!

The Pope built a wall,

the Giza Pyramid built a wall

Fukushima had its new wall back

And as we speak **Dude,**

fuel rods burn at 6000 to 9000 degrees!

Every atom belonging to you belongs to me!

We all gonna be one Fukushima!

We all gonna be one Fukushima!

When the morning comes.

Do the restoration more harm good.

Drop Cesium curds eager into milk.

Japan is going to be sent into the sun

with all the civilizations of the world.

If you want to know why goferments cover up the death of the North Pacific

Stop.

Shut up!

It's not why, it's not why, it's not why.

it's not what, what, what or what.

Why o why o why-o

why o why o way

because because because

the great radioactive

glowworm shows the matin to be near,

no reckoning made.

Where were ye Nymphs when the
remorseless deep
closed o'er my head?

These benzene drippings drip apart.
I thought the Japanese were smart.
They built the Toyota accelerator!
They built the fault lines.
They built near the sea.
They built tank farms on a hill
so drips could go down and melt,
and they built GE!

Tokyo Electric
built reactors as it did
so it would not pay the cost
if it blew a lid

Such effects as hold enmity with the blood of men
ate potassium iodide at Chernobyl and died
but those who ate sea kelp lived.

Reactor Three went down to China
On the Syndrome Train
so did One and Two.

A hundred tons melted in
liability corporate TV
Journalism schools ate the weapon,

Corporate Google GE

Nuke the nukes to personhood,
You won't be charged.

Corporate Radioactivity saves more lives
In spent fuel rods

Pool 4 at Fukushima went
Down swift Hebrus to the Lesbian shore.

I flown down that brandy cask for you sweet
myrtles
in your ivy sere.
That cough's nothing.
It will not kill.

Ye shall not die of a cough!

electric! atomic

Whitman.

Poe.

The body,

The Body.

Like porcupine quills,

each fretful end to end.

Come pluck these berries harsh

and wear your thyroid crude.

Fukushima in **9 million one ton bags**

made necklaces

for all communities round.

24 Empire State Buildings jumped to collect
USoma, Reactor 4
Before it saves the world.

ISIL! ISIl! on the wall!
Revelation again before.

First trump,
take her out and treat her like
a lady.

Second trump,
tell her she's the one that
you've been dreamin' of.

Third trump

take her in your arms and

never let her go.

Don't you know that each half life is

4.2 billion years?

That's the way it goes.

Harrow soul, freeze blood,

two eyes start like stars from their spheres.

Somewhere Shakespeare Principalities

blazon and fall.

Who's going to publish the news?

Murder-like ***Atom***ent.

The one too many world turn dreams
in the mist and the fogbound bush
alone in the violet forest hush
hurry up
the coming rush of dreams is wished for in
the light,
dum-di-dum
the snake is squeezing
its eye is teasing
run snake run
dum-di-dum

the golden age of living
transplants is not yet out.

Oh Waltwald

My tongue, every atom of blood, Form'd

from this soil, this air, Born of parents here.

where each reactor holds 5 million lbs,
all melted down to thousands of cans

Blind Mouse,
Don't drink. Don't Drink, don't drink.

that's the short list, oh!
Pity the H in fish.

Compare five miles girdled round
nine million bags of radioactive beer

compete with cocaine and antidepressants off
the coast.

Young Chinnok in Puget Sound take H
To slow them down.

MaryJane, Aleve and Tylenol.
Paxil, Valium, OxyContin,
Darvon. Nicotine, caffeine, Cipro

Poet of Body and Soul,
how many Hiroshimas depend?

Flee you Vales,
or were you transhumized?

A thousand flee the valleys low.

Your emerald eyes throw Purple on the ground.

Fame as an infirmity in Chernobyl's mind.
Put put 50 Hiroshimas (H) Reactor 4
into mine air.

Japan will get a 10,
North America a 3
Europe a 1, according to Doc Jetstream.

Creeds in abeyance,
we got to fend for truth.

Make your reservations now for fairy tale.
go underground to know they want
to hire English teachers down.

Yale is going to Denver,
so no worry, get your degree.
They go to work in the mortgage fields below,

where Dante works the lame,
halt and blind
scramble at the shearers feast.

Experts by dozens are never wrong.
Detonations, explosions, releases

Grate on your scrannel pipes of straw.

Is this the second Seal or 6th?

Wormwood thought
it was Chernobyl when it fell

but 50 times Hiroshima guy can’t speak.

Wildlife extinction has been achieved.

Here was once the laureate hearse of Lycidas’
gory vis-age.

He did get cancer results from all the nuclear
Homeland tests,
To comfort the sacrosanct in this:
Each reactor had 3450 assemblies.
Each assembly had 80 rods.
Each rod had 18 lbs.
so each reactor had 5 million pounds.

It's laying like an egg.

Chernobyl's equivalent of 400 Hiroshima
bomb 10 days.
Fukushima has 500,000 bombs, so far.

Look homeward angel now and melt.

Its name is written on the forehead of its
Bellowing
that all myths are public dreams,

and dreams
are private myths that stuff
collective unLoosed.

Who you think invented nuclear power, fallen
troops?
Sometimes angels,

sometimes devils.

Hig a pig a pop,

Anaxagoras IAEA exposed all his rods.

Lust to a radiant angel linked, will sate itself.

TEPCO is calling.

The meditation pools are leaking.

Six li'l reactors

was sittin' in lead,

Three was sick

so the other ones said.

Send for the doctor,

and the doctor said,

get them little meltdowns
some absorption lead.

Tepco's little baby
had a meltdown meltdown
Tepco's little baby
on a meltdown sped.

I write to you Krypton 85 to make
California safe.
I write to you horticultural Cesium
to break out strontium tares,
Out of it make smores.

I drink you Tokoy water with BAM Iodine-131.

Bring your 30 million Bq/mz soil mix.

We shall grow a radish.

Deformed daises bring your bow,

bring me your bananas of desire!

Daisy daisy give me your answer do.

Our Hormesis hypothesis is this

-----to cure strontium eat spinach.

In converse get chemotherapy

Sign a waiver.

Experiment your own genes

and 90% children!

Tritium,

strontium 90,

Iodine 131,

Cesium 137

trace 2000 madman elements classified

If all the tracers present in reaction chains
in this snowstorm time
you can't see or feel,

shovel fast, its 15 million year half/life
will outlast
the beaks off Promontory.

If you're a journalist in Japan
report the rapes in France.

Outraged animal carcasses
litter the Fukushima plant.

Billions of baby blue jellyfish "driven by the wind"
Settle on the beaches of Canada and Oregano.

They must not float upon the watery bier
Unwept,
and welter to the parching wind.

We're not supposed to say it.
We're not supposed to say it.
Three million children got disabilities at Chernobyl.

Worried about snow melt?
Man, Tritium prevents ice crystal not the sun
who *tricks his beams with this new-spangled Ore*.

Atoms bio-accumulate immune,
deficiencies spread.
Cancer with parasites,
pathogens prep the body ph electric
Virus Pulse each second, "the wasting
disease."

The Longest Poem Ever Wrote
now leads Finland to its briny waste,

250,000 tons of high grade stuff,
100,000 years of sleep remain in rock.
The Finns took 1700 feet down to BED the
banana!

Bedrock 1.8 billion years would take

the fire to not put out,

stuck down like a treasure not to be found.

like ocean pyramids

Secret societies of doubt

Nuke it out,

It leaves a jar of liver paste

To mark the site

At Onkalo and its spent fuel rods.

This writing see:

Mark but this flea!

It sucked me first,

and now sucks thee,

And cloistered in these walls of jet.

Let not to that, self-murder added be,

Though use make you apt to kill me,
Let not to that, self-murder added be.

That Donne marker
left a feeling of thorns
so one, ever goes
LOOking

To put fire on top the ground so anyone
who dies
Has to dig death not to survive.

I'll wipe away all trivial fond records, all
saws of books,
all forms that youth and observation
copied there

and this commandment alone shall give:

RUN!
Satan inorganic.
Giza's death ray,
fire put to sleep,
never remember thee.

Remember to remember to forever forget.

They worry about the future who made it
what it is,

They sock the hole they stop.
This is the law.
Black metal updates
archive language at each predicted thaw.

Legends whose secret vaults
Worldwide.
Worse than any who ever lived,
repudiate the greed of radioactivity.

Greater deformity each succeeding gen,
2 worse than 1, three worse than two.
Cicadas, butterflies, pink grasshoppers,
Kodiak bears with holes

in their hearts,
Chernobyl heart children with 20-30 Bq/kg
Cesium
heart defects.

Japan heart attacks in youth

Are caused by too much fast food!

Five billion Strontium 90 Bq

goes in the sea EACH DAY.

The perps are planning to fumigate to Mars

Neon Garden 7

Note:

Radiation increases the rate of every other illness, causing premature aging. Cancer death rates are artificially lowered because people die of other diseases first, from their weakened immunity, especially heart attack. See Chernobyl heart, Japanese youth (Nuclear Justice.org). Chris Busby (Fukushima Radiation Threat, 5/15/14) thinks the obviously fake, inverted views of the nuclear industry stem from the attitude of science, especially theoretical physics. If you doubt this go to CERN. He argues that government, academic, scientants have just reversed Galileo's inquisition. His accusers could not believe in the moons of Jupiter, nor in the telescope because such things do not exist. You think them primitive, But EPA, IAEA, NRC, UN, whole nations of Russian and Japan, who have had "accidents" cannot find a correlation of childhood leukemia around nuclear sites. These agencies, which base their analytical paradigm on Hiroshima and infer an equation and formula funded by industry, find Fukushima such a small dose as to be negligible, no matter the thyroid nodules, heart attacks. To support science cancer registries are forbidden to release data. When Three Mile Island's explosion penetrated its containment, it being a calm day, the cloud of radiation settled along the Susquehanna River Valley. Dairy farms were forbidden to sell their milk for some months so they sold it to Hershey's Chocolates nearby, who made it into Cesium, Strontium bars. The highest of radiation exposure among the professions are in farmers, from the dust, but second one Km from the sea from the Sea to Land Transfer. Both causes from inhalation. U238, Lead 210, Lungs are the air filters of the body. Masks? The 50-150 nano meter range of particles in weaponization go thru any mask. Only Chernobyl children with less than 10 Bq per Kg of body weight had normal electro cardiograms (Yuri I. Bandazhevsky. Radioactive Cesium and the Heart). Not just the heart, but the pancreas, thyroid, adrenal gland, and intestinal walls. Children are many times more vulnerable that the 29 year old white

male the industry uses as standard. Women are also twice as vulnerable to these particles than men. Cesium 137 mimics potassium, acting as if it were a macronutrient. (see Helen Caldicot). LLRC.org. Green Audit.org.
Safe limits are set by the military and nuclear industry. Classic hot spots like Hanford, WA, Oak Ridge, Semi Hills, LA, the Irish Sea, the Baltic Sea.

The Implications of The Massive Contamination of Japan With Radioactive Cesium, Steven Starr. The Scary Truth About Fukushima, see Helen Caldicott
State of Morro Bay

Alaska Seabird die off unprecedented. Dana Durnford

Nuclear Evacuations NOT SAFE ANYWHERE On the PLANET: A Gundersen World Uranium Symposium '15

Chernobyl: Consequences of the Catastrophe
Jerry Petermann because corps are declared a person, without a body, hence have no soul or conscience, like machines
FUKUSHIMA.THE SPEECH THAT LET THE CAT OUT OF THE BAG!

While morn touches top and Sun stretches hill, rise, see Fukushima.

Durnford: Everything starved to death but they refuse to mention Fukushima.Check the Nuclear Proctologist: Dana Durnford

Scientists: West Coast bird die-off “is biggest ever recorded” — Stomachs completely empty — “Staggering… Alarming… Unheard of… Never seen anything like it” — “Unprecedented in size, scope, duration” — “Deaths could reach many hundreds of thousands” —

"A host of other freakish phenomena" (VIDEO)
http://tinyurl.com/zaxs2m5

Alaska Seabird Die-Off Excludes Fukushima Again Jan 4th 2016
https://youtu.be/T6MDEeq4BZI

Alaska Dispatch News, Jan 29, 2016: Scientists think Gulf of Alaska seabird die-off is biggest ever recorded… The mass of dead seabirds that have washed up on Alaska beaches in past months is unprecedented in size, scope and duration, a federal biologist said… The staggering die-off… is a signal that something is awry in the Gulf of Alaska http://tinyurl.com/gtu85vu

Heather Renner, Alaska Maritime National Wildlife Refuge: "We are in the midst of perhaps the largest marine die-off ever recorded"… [In Homer] the beaches are "littered" with murre carcasses…
Scientists think Gulf of Alaska seabird die-off is biggest ever recorded http://tinyurl.com/gtu85vu

USGS (pdf), http://tinyurl.com/hpyl8lo Jan 2016: During March through September 2015, at least 25 seabird mortality events were reported across Alaska… The primary avian species reported included common and thick-billed murres, black-legged kittiwakes, horned and tufted puffins, glaucous-winged gulls, and sooty and short-tailed shearwaters… Some of these avian mortalities were concurrent with whale, pinniped, sea otter, and fish mortalities

Alaska Public Radio, Jan 28, 2016: [T]his event will likely be the largest and most widespread on record. And seeing the starving birds dying far inland apparently searching for food is "nearly unheard of,"
Marine Science Symposium – LIVEBLOG – Thursday
http://tinyurl.com/jgpkkwh